Dear Reader,

I'm not a superstitious guy, nor have I ever had many doubts about myself or who I am. But Karen Barnett is changing all that quickly.

I saw her standing alone one morning on the long, broad porch of the old Saxon house. She gave me a start. Nobody, and I mean nobody, goes near that place. I don't believe in ghosts but I do believe in evil, and everything about that house is evil.

As if drawn to her by some outside force, I climbed those porch stairs and found myself looking into the most mesmerizing pair of eyes I'd ever seen. I was unable to shake the uncanny feeling that I had come face-to-face with destiny, and that the world as I knew it would soon come crashing down around me.

Steve Hayes

Nebraska

1. ALABAMA
Full House • Jackie Weger
2. ALASKA
Borrowed Dreams • Debbie Macomber
3. ARIZONA
Call It Destiny • Jayne Ann Krentz
4. ARKANSAS
Another Kind of Love • Mary Lynn Baxter
5. CALIFORNIA
Deceptions • Annette Broadrick
6. COLORADO
Stormwalker • Dallas Schulze
7. CONNECTICUT
Straight from the Heart • Barbara Delinsky
8. DELAWARE
Author's Choice • Elizabeth August
9. FLORIDA
Dream Come True • Ann Major
10. GEORGIA
Way of the Willow • Linda Shaw
11. HAWAII
Tangled Lies • Anne Stuart
12. IDAHO
Rogue's Valley • Kathleen Creighton
13. ILLINOIS
Love by Proxy • Diana Palmer
14. INDIANA
Possibles • Lass Small
15. IOWA
Kiss Yesterday Goodbye • Leigh Michaels
16. KANSAS
A Time To Keep • Curtiss Ann Matlock
17. KENTUCKY
One Pale, Fawn Glove • Linda Shaw
18. LOUISIANA
Bayou Midnight • Emilie Richards
19. MAINE
Rocky Road • Anne Stuart
20. MARYLAND
The Love Thing • Dixie Browning
21. MASSACHUSETTS
Pros and Cons • Bethany Campbell
22. MICHIGAN
To Tame a Wolf • Anne McAllister
23. MINNESOTA
Winter Lady • Janet Joyce
24. MISSISSIPPI
After the Storm • Rebecca Flanders
25. MISSOURI
Choices • Annette Broadrick

26. MONTANA
Part of the Bargain • Linda Lael Miller
27. NEBRASKA
Secrets of Tyrone • Regan Forest
28. NEVADA
Nobody's Baby • Barbara Bretton
29. NEW HAMPSHIRE
Natural Attraction • Marisa Carroll
30. NEW JERSEY
Moments Harsh, Moments Gentle • Joan Hohl
31. NEW MEXICO
Within Reach • Marilyn Pappano
32. NEW YORK
In Good Faith • Judith McWilliams
33. NORTH CAROLINA
The Security Man • Dixie Browning
34. NORTH DAKOTA
A Class Act • Kathleen Eagle
35. OHIO
Too Near the Fire • Lindsay McKenna
36. OKLAHOMA
A Time and a Season • Curtiss Ann Matlock
37. OREGON
Uneasy Alliance • Jayne Ann Krentz
38. PENNSYLVANIA
The Wrong Man • Ann Major
39. RHODE ISLAND
The Bargain • Patricia Coughlin
40. SOUTH CAROLINA
The Last Frontier • Rebecca Flanders
41. SOUTH DAKOTA
For Old Times' Sake • Kathleen Eagle
42. TENNESSEE
To Love a Dreamer • Ruth Langan
43. TEXAS
For the Love of Mike • Candace Schuler
44. UTAH
To Tame the Hunter • Stephanie James
45. VERMONT
Finders Keepers • Carla Neggers
46. VIRGINIA
The Devlin Dare • Cathy Gillen Thacker
47. WASHINGTON
The Waiting Game • Jayne Ann Krentz
48. WEST VIRGINIA
All in the Family • Heather Graham Pozzessere
49. WISCONSIN
Starstruck • Anne McAllister
50. WYOMING
Special Touches • Sharon Brondos

REGAN FOREST

Secrets of Tyrone

Nebraska

Harlequin Books

TORONTO • NEW YORK • LONDON
AMSTERDAM • PARIS • SYDNEY • HAMBURG
STOCKHOLM • ATHENS • TOKYO • MILAN
MADRID • WARSAW • BUDAPEST • AUCKLAND

To Pamela Barnett, for sharing ghosts past and
for enticing the future ghosts of England

HARLEQUIN ENTERPRISES LTD.
225 Duncan Mill Road, Don Mills,
Ontario, Canada M3B 3K9

SECRETS OF TYRONE

ISBN: 0-373-45177-6

Published Harlequin Enterprises, Ltd. 1989, 1993

All the characters in this book have no existence outside the
imagination of the author and have no relation whatsoever to
anyone bearing the same name or names. They are not even
distantly inspired by any individual known or unknown to the
author, and all incidents are pure invention.

Printed in the U.S.A.

Chapter One

A breeze rippled the lace curtains at the windows and crickets chirped in unmowed grass outside. Parted draperies let in what little light was left of the dusk. It was a soft spring evening like a thousand others I had known, but this one was different; an ending. A plaintive voice within me echoed, *You can't go home again. This time is the last time.*

I sat down at the table and untied the string around the dusty box I'd carried down from the attic. Inside were yellowed photographs, a thin, warped high-school annual, letters, a legal document or two, crushed flowers, a silver baby spoon wrapped in pink tissue paper. Tokens of my mother's life. Probably no one had touched this box since Mother's death nine years ago. I had been twenty-one then, in my last year at the university.

Nine years ago my mother, nine days ago I'd lost my father. Strange how the house looked the same as it had when it was filled with life. Only shadows remained now, and shadows were cold, nonliving things.

In the beam of a flashlight—the electricity had already been turned off—I opened a few of the envelopes, thinking how little I knew of my mother's early life. The edge of a photograph protruded from a torn envelope.

When I pulled it out, a flutter of horror began deep in my chest.

With pounding heart, I held the black-and-white photograph under the light. The house! It was the house of my nightmares!

Three stories high, with a wide, railed porch, the white house stood against tall trees. Tall leafy trees, like in my dreams. My hand trembled as I held the picture. This house was real? No, it couldn't be!

There was nothing else inside the plain white envelope. I turned the photo over. On the back was scrawled one word—Tyrone—in gray ink that once had probably been black. The handwriting was small, a woman's perhaps. No date was there, nothing but that one word. I knew I'd never seen this house, and yet if I had never seen it, how could I have dreamed about it over and over again?

Terrifying dreams. Shadows on a staircase. A hand without a body. Wind blowing branches hard against a high window. Ghosts in the wind. Ghosts with faces I could almost see, but never quite. Wind becoming screams becoming sobs. My own? Or someone else's? I had never known. And I had always wondered.

I had wondered all my life what that dream meant. Now, looking at a snapshot of a big white house with flowers in beds across the front, the dream rushed back, its horror choking me. That house! That giant house!

I had to stop myself from crushing the photo in my hand. Crushing it wouldn't make it go away. That damned house existed. Somewhere.

Darkness fell like a cloak over the silent room. Carefully I placed my mother's things back in the box, except for the picture. This I slid into its envelope and into the side pocket of my handbag.

There was a chance the telephone hadn't been disconnected yet. I picked up the receiver and was relieved to hear a dial tone. I dialed a familiar number.

"Aunt Agnes?"

"Karen, dear," she answered. "I hoped you were coming here for dinner."

"I'm sorry. I had to finish going through the house. I found a box of Mother's things in the attic. Can you mail it to me later?"

"Of course. Is there anything else?"

"Just a question. I found a snapshot of a very large white house. It says Tyrone on the back of the picture. Do you know anything about that photo?"

"No. Perhaps your mother lived there as a child. Or it could be just the home of a friend."

"Umm. For some reason Mother kept it in a sealed envelope."

"I don't think it's important anymore, do you, dear? Are you coming to dinner?"

I could hear the sorrow in Agnes Whitney's voice and the strain in my own. "No. I have to fly back to Los Angeles tonight. I've taken what few things I want, except for this box on the dining-room table. I appreciate your taking care of the house sale for me. Keep everything else, or sell it when you sell the house."

"Karen, are you sure? Have you no relative you want to give the things to?"

"You're the closest thing to a relative I have, you know that. You'll always be Aunt Agnes to me."

"I still can't believe your folks are both gone, that the house is empty..."

"Yes," I said gently, remembering Agnes when her hair was jet black instead of gray. Remembering her and my mother drinking tea on the back porch. Remembering their sweet spontaneous laughter.

Agnes's voice strengthened. "You'll write me, won't you, Karen, dear? You'll send me lovely postcards when you travel, like you always did before?"

"Of course, Aunt Agnes."

Closing the window, I felt the soft caress of the lace curtain against my face. I smelled the faint mustiness of dust. I thought of my room upstairs, which looked out on this same view of the back garden. My childhood was this house. My childhood was gone.

In the front hall I unfastened a key from my key ring and stared at it for a few moments through a blur of tears, before I set it on the little table by the door.

Silent goodbyes. I closed the door behind me, tortured by the grim words inside my head: *You can't go home again. You can never go home again.*

THE PHOTO HAUNTED ME day and night. I carried it in my handbag and at the oddest times I felt compelled to take it out and stare at it, and every time I did, a shudder would course through me. Where the devil was that house? Who lived there? And why in the name of heaven was the picture of it driving me to distraction? My curiosity only got worse as I strained to recall details of my recurring dreams—small mind images like pieces of a thousand-piece jigsaw puzzle, all dumped in a heap before me with no clue whatever as to what would be in the finished picture if the pieces were ever assembled. It got to the point where my work began to suffer seriously.

My ability to focus on my jewelry-designing business dwindled as I became obsessed with the house of my nightmares. It was getting impossible to be creative when my mind was so jumbled with the jagged shards of one incomplete and frightening question that seemed to have no answer.

One evening, a week after I returned to California from my small hometown of Milbury, Montana, the thought came that Tyrone might be the name of a town. I took down my atlas from the shelf and found three towns with that name, one in New Mexico, one in Pennsylvania and one in Nebraska. It was information I absorbed with such excitement and foreboding swirling together that I hardly knew where one feeling left off and the other began.

Studying the snapshot propped in front of me on my desk, I eliminated New Mexico because of the enormous trees. And since Pennsylvania was much farther away, Tyrone, Nebraska, was the logical town to check out first. With the dreams taunting me, driving me on, I wouldn't have another restful night or productive day until I had explored every possible avenue.

The greatest advantage to working for oneself is being able to travel at a moment's notice for an unspecified time. My small retail jewelry shop in Santa Monica was managed by Julie Warden, a competent businesswoman and friend. Besides that, the peak buying season was yet to come and my inventory was in good shape. So, two days later I was on the freeway heading east, toward a little town in the rolling hills of western Nebraska, a town I knew nothing about—except that its name was Tyrone.

Forty miles north off the cross-country freeway, the Nebraska state road dipped into a shallow green valley. I'd stayed in an inn overnight and was now completing the last leg of my journey. Or what I'd hoped would be.

To the north, blue hills rose out of the prairie and rolled like ocean waves into the horizon. Wind weaved through the tall wheat. Ahead of me green fields and clusters of tall trees gave evidence that civilization was nearby.

Half-hidden by the wild wheat and wildflowers growing along the edges of the road, a small road sign read Tyrone, Pop. 6,043, but it was another mile before I saw any evidence of a town. A few low buildings appeared first. From the density of trees ahead, I knew a river must run near or through the little prairie town. Everything was unexpectedly green and unnervingly quiet on this clear bright summer morning.

A quarter mile of small highway businesses—gas station, café, a motel, a fishing-equipment store—led to the center of town. The buildings of Main Street were older and larger than I'd expected; most were three stories high. Tyrone impressed me as a town whose face had changed little in half a century.

Odd feelings began to overtake me almost from the moment I entered the business section, but I didn't stop. Without plan or map, I drove on through to the residential streets—wide, paved avenues shaded by great old trees and framed by wide expanses of green lawns. Most of the homes displayed the narrow windows and railed trim typical of houses built in the early decades of this century.

Turning onto a street of exceptionally large homes, all built of wood or of redbrick, I might have appreciated the beauty of the town more had I not been so assaulted by emotional rumblings, the eerie knowledge that I had found the right place. The house of my nightmares would easily fit on this street. I glanced at the photo that lay on the car seat beside me. The trees, the wide front lawn, the porch, the great size of the house—they all looked like Tyrone.

Tense feelings I couldn't identify spun in my head. My being here seemed unreal and at the same time all too real; the feelings made no sense. They spun like spider webs, round and round me, like a trap of gauze. *You're not supposed to be in this town,* something in me warned. While another voice was lifting from the deepest part of me and saying, *Stay . . . stay . . . stay . . . .*

Every street was named for a tree. Elm, Maple, Willow. I turned onto Sycamore Street, and suddenly, looming like an apparition before me, was the house!

My heart nearly stopped. My foot hit the brake. God help me, I thought, this is no apparition! The dream is real!

A heavy cloud suddenly covered the sun and the day seemed to turn ominously dark. Yet, thinking back, I realize there was not a cloud in the sky that summer morning. I must have only imagined the sudden darkness—that cloak of darkness surrounding the house of my nightmares.

It was twice as large as I'd imagined, with an irregular shape typical of many Victorian-style homes. Blinking up in disbelief, I sat in my car, trying to control hideous dream images that were washing through my mind like an angry waterfall. I couldn't stop the images; the dream rushed out, trying to drown me. I saw the stairway again . . . and the still white hand . . . and a second hand reaching from the shadows! No human forms were ever there—just hands! If I was ever to see the faces attached to the hands, would I survive?

My heart pounded against my chest. I felt dizzy.

And weak, as it came to me that this house, this enormous house with its white paint badly chipped, was empty. Deserted! Its high uncurtained windows were filmed with dust, and its lower windows, at least two of which had broken panes, were boarded over. From the look of the place, no one had lived there for years.

Yet the green lawn was freshly mowed. In a flower bed below the porch grew three tall hollyhocks, one with white flowers, another with dark purple flowers, and the other with pink. Their presence provided a gentle blaze of beauty to a stage otherwise sad and empty.

My gaze moved upward to the expansive front porch, to the windows of the second floor and then to the third, until I was squinting through sunlight and tree branches at a small dormer window under the highest eaves of the roof. The sight of that window caused a chill to tremble through me. I closed my eyes and shivered. The house, even boarded up and abandoned, was drawing me to it. Numbly I felt for the handle of the car door and climbed out. I was barely aware of my feet on the pavement as I crossed the street. Something here was so familiar! Was it because I had spent so much time staring at the photograph that this sense of familiarity was creeping over me now? Or could I have been here sometime outside the perimeters of my dreams?

As I crossed the street and stepped onto the stone pathway leading to the front door, and the odd sense of familiarity grew stronger, I desperately combed through every loose fiber of my memory. If my family had ever come here when I was small, they'd never mentioned it. Yet my mother had kept the photograph. Why?

I looked up again at the dormer window on the top floor. That window set my mind images whirring out of control, until a vivid picture skidded to a stop before me. I saw a built-in window seat, a seat with yellow-and-blue cushions; the picture flashed quickly and as quickly disappeared. An image of the staircase pushed through in its place—a stairway, winding down to darkness. In the shadows, a human hand lay near the stair's landing.

Just to keep moving, I had to force the images back to darkness. The windows of the house were like eyes, staring, staring....

I turned away from the staring empty eyes and began to wander aimlessly about the spacious grounds like a lost child. The yard, front and back, was shaded by giant trees—cottonwoods and elms and maples. Lilac bushes grew against the fence. Flower beds were overgrown with grass; only the tall hollyhocks remained, and a few tulips, long past their spring blooming. A tree house nestled high in a great old cottonwood that grew from the yard next door, the branches of which spilled far over the fence, touching the top windows of the empty house. I stared up at the tree house for a long time, amazed that it was so high. Its boards were silvery with age; part of its railing had fallen, yet it looked sturdy enough to hold anyone able to climb up into it.

At the back of the house, the door and the windows were boarded shut, making it impossible to peek in. I returned to the front and climbed the paint-chipped steps. On the ceiling of the wide railed porch were hooks for a porch swing. Some family must have gathered here on summer evenings, with the songs of the squeaking swing and the chirping of crickets and the shrieks of locusts in the trees. Without thinking, I tried the front door, almost expecting it to open. Of course, it didn't; it was tightly secured.

Suddenly, as if it came out of the prairie wind, a thick masculine voice sounded behind me. "The old house hasn't had a visitor in a long time."

Startled, I whirled around. I saw his smile first, which was friendly. Then a shock of mussed, sun-faded brown hair and deep blue eyes, and an unusually handsome suntanned face. He was wearing blue jeans and a blue shirt with the sleeves rolled above the elbows, and cowboy boots. At his side was a large, yellow-white, tail-wagging, cross-bred variety of a Chesapeake retriever.

The stranger and I stared at each other. For a moment time stood still. The breeze stopped blowing and the crickets stopped chirping.

I asked with difficulty, "Is it your house?"

"No."

"Whose is it?"

He stood against the sun, hands in his pockets. "It belongs to a woman named Daphne Hayes."

I looked from the man to the dog who had already lost interest in me and was sniffing around the edges of the porch. "The house is empty. It's been empty for a long time. Is it for sale?"

"I don't think so," he answered with a curious stare. "But no one has ever shown any interest in buying it."

"That's hard to imagine. It's regal and picturesque, and its setting is lovely behind these enormous trees...."

He sat on the porch rail and motioned toward my car. "California license plates. You're a long way from home."

"I was just...driving through...."

The narrowing of his eyes conveyed suspicion. Did I expect him to believe a tourist from California had just happened to cruise along Sycamore Street in a tiny town called Tyrone and had stopped here? Stopped at a house that had nothing unusual about it in this town of huge white houses, except that it had been deserted for some time?

I swallowed self-consciously. "How can I go about finding the owner?"

"The house isn't for sale."

"Why not? If it's been standing empty for so long, why would anyone wish to keep it?"

He shrugged defensively, started to say something, then appeared to change his mind.

"Do you know her?" I asked.

"The owner? Yes."

"Then perhaps you could tell me how to get in touch with her."

"For what reason?"

It was my business, I thought, not his, but it wouldn't serve any purpose to tell him so and risk angering him. He might be a friend of the owner's. Diplomacy might get me further. "I'd like to see inside of this house," I answered politely.

It wasn't easy to be a victim of that steady gaze of his! Bewildering shadows in his eyes formed a smoke screen for his thoughts. No man had ever looked at me the way this man did, and unable to define what was different, I felt a new unease creep over me.

His voice became so soft it sounded like a whisper picked up by a passing breeze. "It isn't for sale. And even if it was, you wouldn't want this house."

"I think I might be a better judge of that."

"One wing is damaged from a fire."

"The outside doesn't show any signs of a fire."

The old railing squeaked when he stood up. "You're not a prospective buyer." He cocked his head sideways. "Are you?"

"I . . . I'm interested in . . . old Midwestern houses. I'd just like to see the inside. Surely—"

"The house is haunted."

I looked him directly in the eye. "Is it?"

He shrugged. "Everyone says so."

"Really? Do you say so?"

"If you're asking whether I've ever seen the ghost myself, nope, I haven't."

"But others have?"

He nodded and started down the steps.

"What did you say the owner's name is? Daphne what?"

"Hayes."

"I assume she's in the telephone directory."

The man's frown signaled his disapproval of my persistence and a hint that contacting the owner might not be a good idea. *Stop looking at me like that,* I wanted to scream. A frown could not stop me; nothing could! If I didn't find the explanation for why my mother would keep a photo of this old house, and why it affected me so, I'd never find peace.

"You'd be wasting your time with Daphne," he said from the bottom of the steps. "She's elderly and very touchy about many things. I don't think she'd open the doors of this house to a stranger."

I met his gaze, only this time he looked away self-consciously, like a man who might be hiding something.

"Are you heading into town?" he asked.

"Yes. To a telephone book. I want to get in touch with this Mrs. Hayes. Unless you're willing to tell me where she lives."

He glanced at his watch. "Daphne is never seen nor heard by anyone before noon. It's too early to try to contact her. But if it's real estate you're interested in, there are one or two other better homes on the market. I can give you the name of an agent who will show you around."

"No. I'm interested in this house. This one."

His glance was like a shooting dart; it almost frightened me. But outwardly he was calm. He stretched, looked around for the dog and said without sincerity, "Well, good luck."

I followed him down the steps, not wanting my only human contact in this town to disappear so quickly. Fumbling for something to say, I muttered, "Your dog seems to enjoy the morning walk."

The man smiled politely. "It's a ritual. I'm on my way to work."

"You walk?"

"Yeah. All five blocks."

Either he was late for work or he was anxious to get away from me, or both, because he made his way quickly down the front walkway without looking back. The dog came bounding around the corner of the house, caught up with its master, and ran in front of him, eagerly leading the way, now that their regular routine was resumed.

Watching him stride away from me, under the leafy shadows of the trees, I experienced a sadness that could only be described as a sense of loss. For all the skepticism in his eyes over my weakly disguised reason for being there, his smile was warm enough to take the chill away. For an instant or two as I stood on the porch steps watching him disappear from view I had the most ridiculous notion that he was not a man, but a ghost.

Long after the man and the dog had disappeared from sight, I stood at the porch rail waiting for him to change his mind and return. Why I expected him to, I had no idea. Then.

Behind me loomed the monstrous house, silent and majestic as a sphinx. I felt a chill at my back as if a cold breeze was blowing from the house, through the door and the windows, even though every opening was sealed. I was frightened. Very frightened.

What is it? I whispered to the silence. *Is it this house? My dreams? Or a man whose eyes are haunting me?*

I did not want the house at my back; I didn't want its riddle or its evil to catch me unaware. Haunted, was it? Were not all deserted houses said to be haunted—especially very large houses like this one? Of course. I should be surprised if it were *not* haunted. But I had to wonder if the alleged ghost had driven people away from here and kept them out! Why else would a house sit abandoned year after empty year?

The chill from a breeze that didn't exist drove me shivering from the porch and down the walkway to the street. This strange street in a strange town. *What did this hideous place have to do with me?*

Dazed, I got back into my car, remembering the motel on the road that led into town. No plan had taken form in my mind as I headed back toward the highway, but determination propelled me. I was going to get into that house! I had been inside it in my dreams, and I had to know if in life it looked the same. I prayed it did not. I prayed that my flashes of mind images could never ever be real.

And yet the house was real. Some explanation must exist! I was more frightened of finding the truth than of failing to find it, but the truth tugged and pulled at me with such force, there was no going back now. I'd found the domain of my gruesome nightmares, and I would not leave this town until I'd faced what lay behind the bolted doors of that house!

Constructed of redbrick with white wood trim, the Country Inn Motel sat under shade trees, forming a quarter-circle around a grassy lawn. The structure had the look of the 1940s, but it had been well maintained during its long lifetime.

The proprietor, who checked me into the motel, was so friendly, I was tempted to ask her what she knew of the big empty house on Sycamore Street, but something held me back. It would be wiser not to call too much attention to the reason I was in town, because people would ask questions in return and I didn't have a believable explanation. To get information, one needed credibility; I had begun to realize how strange I must have sounded to the stranger at the house. No wonder he'd been suspicious.

My motel room was small but pleasant and decorated in shades of mint and green, which was a great relief after crossing half the United States hopping from one rust-and-orange motel room to another. The rust color had begun to corrode my dreams and worsen my recurring insomnia.

In the drawer of the bedside table was a thin local phone book. I sat on the edge of the bed, trying to shake off qualms from my inner self that fell barely short of warnings. Only one Hayes, Steve, was listed—Daphne's husband, perhaps. When there was no answer at that number, I scribbled down the address, frustrated by my lack of success.

It wouldn't hurt to make sure it was the right number. I dialed information. To my surprise, the operator gave me a different number for Daphne Hayes.

This time a woman answered in a voice neither old nor young.

"My name is Karen Barnett," I began. "I'd like to speak with Daphne Hayes."

A long uncomfortable pause ensued before she answered, "Yes?"

"I understand you own a house on Sycamore Street—the empty house." I waited for confirmation. There was none, only silence.

Since I'd been told it was doubtful the house was for sale, I had decided on a different approach. "I just happened to see the house as I drove through town, and since I'm very much interested in old houses, I inquired about the owner's name in hopes you'd allow me to view the lovely old home. It's for...research."

The woman paused again. "What did you say your name is?"

"Karen Barnett."

I sensed hostility in her silence.

"I'm sorry," the woman replied at last. "I can't allow anyone in the house. It's in serious disrepair."

"But surely I could just look at it...look around a bit."

The voice had become colder and more impatient. "I'm afraid it's quite impossible."

I asked, "Is the house for sale?"

"No."

"Why not? It...it's a very beautiful home."

"Because I have no desire to sell it."

Afraid she was about to hang up on me, I tried pleading. "Please, Mrs. Hayes. All I want to do is look at the interior—"

"It's the ghost, of course," she said. "Others have asked to investigate the ghost. It's all utter nonsense. The house is not safe and I want no strangers snooping about in there."

"Can you tell me why it has sat vacant for years?"

"I simply haven't had the inclination to restore it."

"But—"

"This silly ghost business is exaggerated," the woman interrupted. "But I want no one in the building because it is unsafe."

She hung up. I knew it was no use to call again. I had hit a wall.

Nothing made sense. Except maybe the ghost. Ghosts don't make sense as a rule, but this one did. A powerful local belief in that ghost was the only available explanation for the abandonment and neglect of such a beautiful house.

That ghost was the reason Daphne Hayes had acted so threatened by my request, I was sure. Did people really fear ghosts that much? Or in the case of this one, did they have some reason to?

Chapter Two

While I changed from shorts and T-shirt into a white blouse and pale blue denim skirt, I conjured up a more acceptable excuse for being in Tyrone. By the time I had walked back to the wood-paneled office of the Country Inn Motel, my story was plausible, despite my discomfort with such blatant lying.

The woman behind the desk set aside her knitting and smiled. "How can I help you—" she glanced at her register "—Miss Barnett?"

"I'm interested in haunted houses," I began. "For an article I'm working on. There's a large abandoned house here in Tyrone on Sycamore Street. Can you tell me what you know about it?"

The woman's sincere smile put me at ease. "The old Saxon house. It hasn't been lived in for decades."

"I've heard it's haunted," I prompted.

"Haunted as they come."

"Is that the reason no one lives there?"

Her attention focused on a gurgling percolator behind the counter, but her manner indicated she was willing to talk. She asked, "Would you like a cup of coffee?"

"The coffee smells wonderful. Yes, thank you."

She poured out two cups and motioned me to one of the two cushioned chairs in the small lounge. We took a moment to settle in. "The truth is, I always did assume no one lived in the Saxon house because of the ghost." She handed me a steaming cup of black coffee. "The place was empty when we came here fifteen years ago and nobody in town talks about it much. The house just sits there like something grown to the land, like a hill or a tree. It just sits there and nobody has ever told me why."

"You haven't been curious?"

The gray-haired woman took a sip of her coffee. "As I understand it, the owner of that house is as eccentric as they come. Daphne Hayes, her name is. She'd be the person you'd want to talk to."

"Do you know anything about the last people who lived in the house?"

"Not a thing. They were gone before I came."

From the low counter, I picked up a business card and read aloud, "Country Inn, Tyrone, Nebraska, Wanda and Clancy Clark, owners. Are you Wanda Clark?"

"I am. Clancy, my husband, takes mornings to sleep or fish and works evenings when I'm watching television. We alternate shifts. That's the secret of a business like this—alternating shifts. Along with hiring a maid to do up the rooms."

"Mrs. Clark—"

"Oh, call me Wanda."

"Wanda, if there's a haunted house in town, people must talk about it. Is it supposed to be haunted by one ghost, or more than one?"

The woman scratched the top of her gray head. "Well, now. I've only heard tell of one ghost. Every now and then somebody makes mention of the ghost over there, but it's been going on for so many years, you know, that folks don't get particularly excited over it anymore.''

"What happens?"

"I can't say as I know, really. I always assumed it was just so much hot air blowing by, because the house is boarded shut. Nobody goes in there, none that I ever heard about. So if nobody's in there, I don't know what could've been seen, do you?"

"It seems incredible to me that hauntings aren't talked about more in a town this size."

Wanda Clark smiled. "Tyrone's an odd sort of town, if I do say so. They close up to outsiders. There are secrets, too. Clancy and me have been here fifteen years and we got friends here, but we've never been accepted by the old core. They're a tight group made up of the town's pioneer stock. The owner of that Sycamore Street house, Daphne Hayes, is part of the inner circle. In fact she's probably the most powerful person in Tyrone, and that house is just looked on as part of her property. No newcomer who's rich enough to buy that place would be accepted by this town's upper echelon, and none of *them* wants the Saxon house." She looked up at me over the rims of her glasses. "I don't think you're going to find out much about that place. Not unless the old lady tells you."

The little bell on the door rang as a teenage boy entered with a delivery. The motel owner directed him to the kitchen in the back.

I stood up. "Thank you, Wanda. You've been a big help."

She said, "On TV those professional journalists are good at digging up their stories. I think you'll have to be as good if you want to know the truth about that house."

I walked back into the warmth of the summer morning. There was no cloud in the sky and birds were singing. The air was clean and fragrant like that of my own hometown, and it made me remember the carefree summer days of my childhood. Leisure hours spent along the creek looking for croaking frogs. Songs of birds, the meadowlark, the elusive thrush. For some moments I escaped into nostalgia, missing those magical summer mornings of the past, which were gone forever and yet so incredibly alive.

Wanda Clark had been more helpful than she knew, because her information gave me the advantage of caution I might not otherwise have exercised. Intuitively I knew she was right about secrets surrounding that house. No small town was without its secrets, of course, its scandals, its brand of royalty.

Hell, I thought. I was sure one of the secrets of that house was *me*. So how would I go about learning how my mother acquired that picture, and then left it for posterity?

I had one thing—a name. Saxon. After driving to the courthouse I searched through public records, trying to find out anything I could about the Saxon name and the house on Sycamore. The search took hours and turned up next to nothing. All I found was a one-line record of a house purchase by Daphne Hayes. From that brief entry, I learned the house had been purchased twenty-five years ago at public auction, which meant the previous owner had either gone bankrupt or had died without heirs. Why would anyone want to purchase a house only to let it go to ruin? The woman was eccentric, all right.

According to the man with the unforgettable blue eyes who had surprised me on the steps of the house, part of the inside had been damaged by fire. Perhaps the house had caught fire after it'd been sold, and Mrs. Hayes simply had never been willing to spend the money needed to restore it.

What needled me was the escalating conviction that talking to people around here wasn't going to help me much, even if I knew which people to talk to, which I didn't. I needed to see the house. Inside. I would never put either my conscious mind or my dreams to rest until I knew what mysterious force had drawn me to a haunted house and a town full of reticent citizens.

I'd tried to think of every possible explanation, and I was still trying. Suppose I had seen that photo when I was a child at the same time someone recited a frightening story? That would explain my recurring nightmare.

But then again, in my dreams I vividly saw the house's interior. And if the interior was as I had dreamed it, then as far as I was concerned, there was no explanation except that I'd been there before. But when?

Sitting on a bench in the wide hall of the old courthouse in Tyrone, I went over it all again. With my head back against the wall and my eyes staring up at the high ceiling, I analyzed my situation. The old woman, Daphne Hayes, was determined to keep people out of that house. And my determination to get in was only heightened. There had to be a way.

If only I could talk to her in person.

I dug into my purse for my little notebook on which I had scribbled the address of the only other Hayes in the phone book. In such a small town, this person was bound to be a relative. People were friendly in this part of the world; it shouldn't be difficult to obtain the address of the haughty Mrs. Hayes from a family member. Surely the old woman would listen to me if I were to plead my case in person, even if I had to let down the barriers and tell the truth about why getting into her house was so important to me.

Steve Hayes lived at 600 West Maple Street. It was worth a try. Anything was worth a try.

I hated knocking on the doors of strangers, but back in my hometown of Milbury, people thought nothing of it. This wasn't Los Angeles, after all; this was a quiet little town the size of Milbury. I remembered that Maple Street was near Sycamore. Six hundred West would be in the same neighborhood as the Saxon house.

The eerie feeling of unreality that had hit me in this area earlier assaulted me again. This time, I turned onto a street of smaller homes, mostly of red and yellow brick—well-maintained places and typical of homes of the thirties, set close together with deep front lawns.

Children's voices and the barking of a dog broke the summer silence on Maple Street. Six-hundred West Maple turned out to be a redbrick house with white shutters and a stone chimney. It was one of the few homes on the street that had no flower beds along the front walk.

I pulled up to the curb and walked up the driveway to the front door. I rang the bell several times. There was no answer. Disappointed, I went back to my car. Even before I started the engine, I felt a powerful tug toward Sycamore Street. The Saxon house pulled me like a huge magnet. I made a U-turn in the wide empty street, and four short blocks later, I found myself there again.

That damned house spoke to me in a language I could not understand. It whispered and sighed, and sometimes it screamed, and would not leave me in peace.

Once again, I walked up its front pathway under the trees. My mind played tricks on me, blurring reality while I followed my feet to the front porch as if I were a guest, awaited. As if there were glass and open curtains at the windows and voices from within. As if the door stood gleaming white and open. Blended with yearning, my imagination made it real.

My steps echoed on the wooden floor of the porch. Behind the two heavy locks on the front door were my nightmares. I was angry that the house dared keep me out! Its doors and its hideous secrets had been open to me in my dreams. Why not now?

Frustrated, I stepped down off the porch and onto the lawn. The grass was spongy under my feet. I paused under the tree house, staring up at it until I was dizzy from the motion of wispy clouds whirling on a high erratic wind. The great old tree that housed it shaded both yards, but it grew from the soil of the lawn next door. Boys must have built that sturdy tree house years ago.

Walking about the spacious back yard, I became overpowered by the feeling that the house was pushing me away. "Make up your mind!" I muttered at its silent windows as if the house was a living thing and could hear me. "One minute you draw me with some awesome force, and the next minute you repel me!" Mixed feelings of love and horror assailed me in this place. If I had been confused before I came, I was losing my foothold on sanity now. I don't know how long I wandered there before the sadness of the house began to overtake me. I seemed to be absorbing its sadness as if I were a part of it.

"Poor house," I said aloud, plopping myself down on the top step of a little side porch. "You stand so pitifully wrapped in your memories—decaying, deserted, unloved. No house deserves such a fate!" And I asked, *Who are you? Why do I know you?* And I wondered if the house, like me, had a heartbeat.

Two figures blurred through my teary eyes. They came around the corner, the dog running ahead of the man. Neither of them seemed surprised to see me sitting on the tiny side porch step, chin in palm.

"I thought you might be here," he said.

He wore the same clothes he'd had on this morning, jeans and boots, with his sleeves rolled to elbows. His eyes were even bluer than I remembered. I asked, "Why did you think I'd be here?"

"I thought about you today and wondered if you'd contacted Daphne. It took a while for it to sink into my head that seeing this house was important to you for some damn reason. I can't figure why. I don't even care why. But I figured you probably got nowhere with the old woman, and I knew you'd be back."

"You're right, I got nowhere with her. She practically hung up on me."

This didn't seem to surprise him. He was gazing at me, hands in his pockets, when he said, "You ruined my day."

"What?"

"By nature I'm not a curious man. But you...turning up out of the blue at this house. The fear in your eyes when you looked at it. The place scares you, and yet you insist you want to see its interior. My antennae says something's wrong."

I stood up. "Isn't everyone afraid of haunted houses and fascinated at the same time? The owner says it isn't safe. Did she mean the ghosts, even though she insisted the ghost stories are nonsense?"

"She always uses the excuse that the house is decaying to keep people out."

"And the real reason?"

"I wouldn't know."

His voice was cold, untrusting, because I so blatantly avoided his questions. It was important to me not to alienate him, even though I couldn't sharply define my reason. Something about him, and the fact that he had come back here looking for me. He distracted me with his eyes at a time when I needed all my wits about me. My voice softened until I was almost pleading. "You said you knew her. Could you talk to her? I know it's a lot to ask, but I'd be so grateful."

"It would do no good."

"Please?"

His gaze met mine. "Daphne is a reasonable woman about . . . some things. But she won't discuss this house with anyone."

"I have to keep trying! I have to."

Giving me a puzzled look, he sat down on the step next to me. "We haven't officially met. What's your name?"

"Karen Barnett. I'm from Santa Monica."

"Steve Hayes," he said.

"What? Hayes? You're—"

"Yeah, I'm a Hayes. Daphne is my grandmother."

I stared at him. The house I'd stopped at earlier—the redbrick house on Maple Street—was his!

"I take care of the yard," he was saying, "and generally keep an eye on things. That's why I was here this morning."

"Why didn't you tell me?"

"Tell you what? That my grandmother owned it? I saw no reason to. Her owning this house has nothing to do with me, except as a major irritation. I hate this place."

"But you help her with it." She looked at the manicured lawn. The flower beds needed weeding, but that was it.

"I rarely go inside. The house gives me the creeps."

"Why?" I shifted nervously. My shoulder brushed his. The contact of my body with his sent dull shards of awareness through me—awareness of his strength, his masculinity. More so because he could admit he was half-afraid of this house.

He was concentrating on his boot heel digging at the dirt below the bottom step.

I pressed on. "It gives you the creeps because it's haunted?"

"I don't know...Karen. To all appearances, the house is dead. But its spirit isn't dead. There's something in there, something that bothers the hell out of me. I get a bad feeling in there."

When he moved his foot, his thigh brushed mine. A small shiver coursed through me, and I didn't know whether the shiver was caused by his touch or his words, or both. And I didn't know whether he had touched me on purpose.

I asked softly, "Could you have let me in this morning?"

"No. I didn't have a key."

"Didn't? Are you saying you have one now?"

"There'd be hell to pay if Daphne ever found out I let anybody in here."

My heart leaped. "You *do* have a key! Mr. Hayes, please!"

"Steve."

"Okay. Steve. Please let me inside."

He looked at me quizzically. "I don't understand you, Karen Barnett, and it's obvious you don't want me to."

"That isn't true. It's just... hard to explain. You see, my mother, who died some years ago, kept a picture of this house in a sealed envelope among her most personal possessions. I didn't find the picture until recently, after my father died, but I have reason to believe this house was important to my mother. I have certain...certain memories of it...well, of something to do with it...." I reached into my handbag, drew out the photo and handed it to him.

Only after studying the photo for some time did he answer, "It's the same house, all right. You're trying to trace your family history, are you?"

"Something like that."

He stood up. "I don't know what the inside of this house could possibly tell you, but I do have the key with me. I picked it up because I was sure you'd be back."

My heart was thundering as we walked around to the front. "It was...kind of you to bring the key."

"Taking somebody in this damned house isn't an act of kindness. I've even heard people say it has a curse on it and anybody who goes inside will instantly regret the intrusion into...into the domicile of the ghosts."

"Good Lord! No wonder it hasn't sold."

Steve smiled. We walked up the steps. "For all I know Daphne started the curse rumor herself," he said. "It's the sort of thing she would do."

"I think I'd like to meet your grandmother."

"No, I doubt you would."

The same key opened both locks on the door. Steve pushed the door open with his foot and gestured with a tiny bow. "Don't say you weren't warned."

Heart fluttering, I entered a spacious foyer. On my right was a carved wooden stairway that curved up toward a window on a high landing. Leaves had been etched into the wood casing—exactly the same as in my dreams!

I went dizzy and weak and it took all the willpower I had to force myself to walk toward those stairs. The walls kept the bottom steps in deep shadow and the shadows shivered with something almost alive. Yet there was nothing there.

Barely able to take it in, I had to close my eyes. But that was worse. A second of darkness behind my lids was all it took for the familiar picture to appear—the white silent hand wearing a sparkling ring . . . no, a hand without a ring. Sparkles of red, phantoms of gray. First the ring was there and then it was not. . . .

I reeled. Steve's voice came from behind as he rushed toward me.

"Are you all right?"

I looked at him blankly, too numbed by the interior of my visions to comprehend the concern in his voice. I must have staggered, because he touched my arm to steady me.

"What's wrong?"

"Nothing's wrong," I whispered.

He scowled at my lie.

I wanted to grab his arm for some solid protection, but I didn't dare. After pleading with him to let me in here, I was determined not to make a fool of myself. He didn't deserve a quaking clinging woman as a reward for the favor he'd shown me. And anyway, there was something so unsettling about this man that any contact with him set off a rush of unfamiliar and incomprehensible emotions.

Backing away from the frightening shadows of the staircase, I gazed about the high-ceilinged foyer. A large wood-paneled archway led to the living room in the south wing. On the north side, French doors opened into the formal dining room.

"I don't see any signs of a fire."

"It was in the back of the house on the ground floor. The kitchen and breakfast room and a back bedroom were gutted, but the fire was stopped before the whole place went up in flames.''

I stepped into the living room, with its faded patches on pale rose wallpaper where huge pictures had once hung. Beyond it was a many-windowed sitting room. Even though the day was warm, there was a chill in the house—an evil chill. Our footsteps echoed. Dust on the hardwood floors was thick enough for footprints, and no prints other than those of Steve's boots and my summer sandals were here. Our breathing seemed to reverberate across the emptiness. We breathed silence and dust.

I circled through the south rooms, but my feet, ignoring the awful pounding in my heart, didn't want to stay away from the stairway. Soon, I was standing at the bottom once again, looking up.

"Be careful of the stairs," my guide warned. "It's pretty steep, and for all I know the floors could be weakened by termites, although I've never see any signs of termites. I don't trust this house, though, so just . . . be a little careful of your step. I'll go first."

In silence, he led me up the stairs. My legs were trembling. I hated to touch the banister; it felt as cold as ice, but I had to hang on to keep my balance. My dream pictures faded and then rushed back so vividly that I was walking in the nightmare once again. The present kept rolling back in waves, and then leaving again. I felt dizzy, almost ill.

At least the form of the man in front of me, silhouetted in the light from the high upper window, was real and solid. Steve Hayes's presence held me to the reality of the moment. Gave me courage. I don't think I could have entered that house alone—not that first time, anyway— and I know I couldn't have climbed alone up these creaking stairs. The farther we ascended, the more I trembled with fright.

A shuffling sound below startled me. The yellow dog had circled back from his exploration of the back yard and found the front door open. He was halfway up the stairs already when Steve muttered something about his pet's ill manners and then stepped aside to let the dog pass. The retriever, undaunted, bounded up ahead of us.

I asked, "Why is your dog in such a hurry? Does he hear something up there?"

"Nah. Unless a squirrel has come in through a broken window. Skipper would rather snoop around than eat. He likes to sniff out an adventure."

"Or a ghost?"

"Or a ghost," he confirmed.

At the second-floor landing, Steve started down the hallway, but I didn't follow him. Some force too powerful for me to resist was pulling me on up the stairs—toward the third story. I kept climbing while the noises from old nightmares filled my head. Music, like someone singing—softly at first, then louder as I approached the top of the stairs.

Halfway down the hall, Steve turned around and saw me still on the stairs, blinking up through slants of light toward the top. "What are you looking at, Karen?"

"The high window. What's on the third floor?"

"The rooms up there are smaller and oddly shaped—gabled." He caught up with me. "Are you sure you want to go all the way up? The ghost is up there."

"What do you mean?"

"It's said the ghost is always seen at one of those high windows."

"Always seen from outside? Has anyone seen anything from inside the house?"

"No. No one has been in here." He brushed my shoulder gently as he moved ahead of me to take the lead again. Protectively.

The top-floor hall was very narrow and twisting, under the curves of the roof. "This is the spookiest house I've ever seen!"

He attempted to calm me. "If you hear something, don't panic. It'll just be a squirrel."

My own voice echoed back through the emptiness. "I'm glad you and your dog are here. I'm . . . scared . . ."

"Of what?"

"Of . . . of . . ." I couldn't say it aloud! What I feared was that I was about to come face-to-face with the horror of my nightmares. But I couldn't explain it to him. Not now . . . not here. My whole body was shaking.

Some unseen force was guiding me through the shadowy hall. I walked past one room, barely glancing in. On my right, on the northeast corner of the house, would be the room with the dormer window. It was that room I headed for.

I paused in the open doorway of the northeast room, staring in at faded, pale blue walls and hushed blue shadows. The only straight wall was papered with a design of tiny yellow-and-white flowers against a background of blue. White window seats stretched under each of the two gabled windows, through which watery light streamed.

Suddenly the room became fuzzy. Then clear again, but now it looked so different! Now thin white curtains were blowing in the breeze of the open windows. I caught a fractured glimpse of blue-cushioned benches with yellow flowered pillows under each of the dormer windows. When I blinked, the curtains disappeared. The blue-and-yellow pillows disappeared. The benches were still there, in the window alcoves, but they were cushioned only by layers of dust.

Why did I know this room? Why did its very walls whine with secrets I could almost hear, almost see?

I don't know how long I stood in the doorway before I realized Steve was staring at me with eyes that conveyed far more than curiosity. I must have been acting very strangely, standing there trancelike.

Hands in his jeans pockets, he moved past me into the odd-shaped room, walked to the north window and stood looking down through the tree branches over the side lawn. The branch the tree house sat on was so close to the window a person could almost climb out onto it. Steve stood with a blank expression on his face, as if he had noticed the big branch for the first time in his life. I knew he was suspicious of my odd behavior. How could I be truthful with him about what was happening when I couldn't explain it even to myself?

Still gazing out through the dirty rain and dust-smeared window, Steve asked, "Why this room?"

My eyes moved from the blank, pale blue walls to the expanse of his wide shoulders. "I don't know why. Something just seemed to...draw me here."

"Umm. The ghost."

I chilled. "Why do you say...ghost like that?"

"This little room is where a ghost is always seen. From these two windows. I don't see how you could have known that." He turned around to look at me. "If your mother had a photo, maybe you've been here before."

"No, I haven't. I'm sure I haven't. Steve, a...ghost is supposed to haunt this particular room?"

He sat on the window seat, in the thick dust. "Do you believe in ghosts?"

"No...I don't think so. Do you?"

He smiled, shaking his head. The dog was running up and down the hall, in and out of the upper rooms, but he wouldn't enter this room. He looked in, cocked his head and then ran on.

"What's the matter with you, Skipper?" his master asked. "Something in this room that spooks you?"

"Maybe it's me," I offered in a weak voice.

"Of course not. It's the room. Dogs sense things we can't, I'm convinced of it. My canine friend there, by the way, is Skipper Flash, son of a champion Chesapeake retriever and a traveling vagabond of unknown origin."

"Does he go wherever you do?"

"My dog goes just about wherever he wants."

I smiled. "A town without leash laws."

"We have a leash law. That is, I think we do. It's for the other dogs."

He sat back against the window, one knee up, stroking his chin. There were small frown lines across his forehead. "Karen, if you don't believe in ghosts, why are you so nervous?"

I glanced away. "It must be the weird sounds in here...."

"What sounds?"

"That sort of . . . of singing. Don't you hear it?"

"All I hear are the leaves brushing against the window. If you mean the birds singing outside—"

"No, not the birds. Voices . . ."

Frantic, I pressed my hands over my ears to stop the voices from getting any louder. It didn't help. The sounds were not in the house; they were in my head.

He watched me in a silence so heavy I could scarcely bear the pressure of it. Nervous perspiration was making me feel hot and sticky. I knew I must seem an absolute fool.

And yet, to my surprise he was patient. Not his eyes, but his voice, as he sat quite still on the window seat.

"What do you know about this house?" he asked.

"I know nothing about it."

"I don't believe you. You've been trembling since you walked in the door."

I tried to meet his eyes and couldn't. "Something terrible happened here, didn't it?"

He turned back to the window.

"Didn't it?"

His voice came back so softly I could barely hear the words. "I don't know what happened here."

Hiding my frustration was getting more and more difficult. Voices beat in my head; terror beat in my heart. Weakness caused my legs to feel numb. I wanted to run, but there was no place to run to, except down those terrible stairs.

And it was worse down there. The voices on the lower floor were not singing; they were screaming.

And the way Steve Hayes, a stranger, was looking at me was beginning to scare me, too.

He continued to rub his chin, like someone who was trying to fit a puzzle together. "It's impossible," he said finally.

"What is?"

"That you've been here before."

I took a step back. Behind me in the doorway, the dog was panting loudly. "I told you I've never been here. Why do you look at me so strangely?"

His deep blue eyes looked hard into mine. "No one ever comes here, Karen. No one. This house has been empty since before you were born."

Chapter Three

I turned my back to him and to the pale blue room that had been occupied, in the span of my lifetime, only by the ghost, in darkness, and I, in my childhood dreams. "Let's go down," I said. Steve rose and followed me out.

At the top of the stairs I paused, feeling queasy. Below, beyond the gray misty light from the high window, the slumbering shadows seemed to move—very slightly, as if they were breathing. The staircase coiled downward like a serpent whose eyes sought cover of darkness out of the range of my vision. The stairs felt eerily alive; they seemed to move under my feet. I gritted my teeth and tried to keep my balance while I made myself take that first step down. Steve was behind me, patient and silent; I was glad he couldn't see the terror turning to tears in my eyes.

As I looked down from the middle landing, my nightmare flashed and shimmied before me. Over the curve of bending stairs lay death! Death personified by a white still hand, and everything else hidden by the railings and the wall and the black, breathing shadows. Blinding sparkles of jewels—diamonds the color of tears, rubies the color of blood, glittering, moving...

Drowning in a flood of screams, I was so dizzy that a firm hold on the banister was all that kept me from falling.

"Be careful!" his voice boomed from behind me, but it didn't sound like his voice, or the voice of any human. It was shrill and high and echoed hideously against the confining walls of the stairwell. "Don't go any farther!" the voice wailed. "Don't go down...don't go down..."

An icy hand grabbed my shoulder. His hand. Steve's.

Steve Hayes was throwing his voice, making himself sound like a ghoul! I turned abruptly and shrieked, "Stop it! Why are you doing that?"

"Because you looked like you were about to lose your balance. I thought I'd have to catch you."

The voice was human again. "Who are you?" I cried.

"What's the matter, Karen? All I said was be careful. Here, give me your hand. You don't look too steady on your feet."

"You told me not to go down the stairs!"

"Why would I tell you that? Do you think I like it here? I told you outside that I hate this damned house. What the devil is with you? Still hearing voices?"

How could I answer? Either the house really did have a resident ghost or the voices were coming from my head! Memories of nightmares?

At the bottom landing, everything was still. Even the shadows lay as silent as sleep. The screams in my head had changed to sobs and had finally faded into the silence, too. Steve released my hand.

I didn't know whether it was confusion or understanding beneath his silence, because I wasn't sure what I had done on the stairs, other than accuse him of throwing his voice, an accusation he didn't seem to understand.

Steve looked up at his dog, who was having difficulty getting down the steep stairs. "Come on, Skipper! You've conquered worse obstacles than this."

Painstakingly, determined not to be left behind, the dog eased his way down to safety.

I looked about the main-floor foyer. "The kitchen is in the back."

"Yes. Burned, I told you. Maybe we shouldn't go into that wing. It isn't, uh, safe . . ."

"I want to see it."

"I don't."

"Then I'll go."

"No. Don't . . . not alone."

He pushed open the French doors slowly, reluctantly, and we entered the large blue-and-white dining room. On the far side, where a door opened to the kitchen, the walls were darkened by smoke. The door frame was charred.

There were gaping holes in the kitchen where the appliances had been removed. Some of the cabinet work was burned, and the walls and floor were blackened.

"Does it still smell like smoke, or am I only imagining it?"

"It smells like smoke to me," he answered. "Maybe we're both imagining it."

From the kitchen window was a view of the back yard. I visualized a woman standing at that window preparing an evening meal while twilight crept across the sky. She might have heard the voices of children playing outside. She might have been listening to music on the radio as she worked, or to the voice of her husband from the breakfast nook across the room. It could be any household family scene.

Steve stood in the kitchen doorway. "Seen enough? Let's go."

"There's another room, behind the kitchen."

"That back room was gutted by the fire. There's nothing to see." His protest was a little too quick. His gaze shifted uncomfortably.

I didn't care at that point whether he followed me into the charred back room or not; I was inside this house and I was going to see it all.

He was right, though; there wasn't much to see. The room was long and rectangular with five windows in a line across one wall. All but one of the windows was blackened by smoke and the walls were scarred by the long-ago flames.

It was a hideous room! Burned and dead and awful. My first impulse was to turn away. I paused in the doorway, feeling a strange chill.

From the kitchen Steve asked, "Do you feel it?"

"What?"

"The cold."

"Yes. What is it?"

A wave of cold permeated the air of that room, as if the temperature had dropped suddenly and drastically.

"I don't know what it is," he answered.

I turned to look at him. "This cold has nothing to do with temperature. It has to do with evil. Steve, this room reeks of evil!"

"Yeah," he said from the kitchen. It was obvious he had no intention of stepping one foot inside the cold fire-scorched room. He'd been in here before, I thought.

We both stood dead still—I was at the entrance, and he was far back, behind me.

"No need to go in there, Karen."

I shuddered. "What do you know about this room?"

"Not a damn thing. I never come in here."

"Is it supposed to be haunted, too? There's something so evil here—"

"Dammit, Karen, I don't believe in ghosts!"

"No? Then what's the matter with you?"

There was a look in his eyes that had not been there before, a look I didn't like. His jaw had tightened, and he would not take one step toward me.

"Do you want an honest answer? It's the evil you feel here. I feel it, too, and I don't like it. Haven't you seen enough?"

"Yes . . ." I answered hesitantly. "But wait, tell me where that boarded door leads. Is it an outside exit?"

"Yeah, to the small porch you and I were sitting on earlier, at the side of the house."

When I turned around, he was no longer there. I could hear his footsteps moving away from me, toward the front of the house. I hurried to catch up with him.

"Steve, something horrible happened in that back room, didn't it?"

"Nothing that I ever knew about."

"Then why do you react so strongly to it?"

"I don't know." His voice was short. "Maybe the damn thing's haunted."

While I had clearly seen the carved stairwell and the blue dormer room in my nightmares, I hadn't seen anything that resembled the charred room behind the kitchen. Yet I might as well have, considering the effect it had on me. And its effect on Steve Hayes was obviously even stronger. He didn't even try to hide his extreme discomfort.

I said, "I must not keep you any longer. It's getting late and you're probably anxious to get home."

"Anxious to eat, more importantly." He thrust his hands into his back pockets and looked around for his dog who hadn't followed us into the north wing of the house. "It's a short walk into town," he continued. "How about walking in with me and getting a bite to eat? It's too early for dinner, but I missed lunch and I'm not at my best when I'm hungry. I want to talk to you."

"I was afraid you might."

He cocked his head and squinted at me. "You want to know more about this house. And I want to know more about you and what connection you could possibly have to it. So, we'll talk."

I nodded agreement, dreading talk, because the truth wasn't believable, yet I couldn't avoid the truth and learn nothing.

"Let's get the hell out of here, Karen."

We were in the foyer now. Crossing the lower landing, I, too, felt an uncontrollable urge to get out of this house.

Steve yelled, "Skipper, come on! Let's go. Where is that crazy dog?"

Skipper materialized at the summons, carrying something in his mouth. His master took time to investigate. "What have you got there, old boy?" he asked, nudging the dog on the nose. Steve was rewarded with a small, wet rubber ball, the kind children use for playing jacks. "Hey, this is quarry for a great hunter?" He tossed the ball into the air. The dog leaped up like a shot of electricity and came down with his tail wagging wildly.

"He caught it!" I exclaimed. "How did he do that? It was so fast I didn't even see him connect with the ball!"

"Skipper's reflexes are faster than any dog I've ever seen. He'll retrieve anything that's flying. That is, anything but a bee. Right, Skip? He caught a flying bee once—just once."

Excitedly the dog spit the ball into Steve's hand again. Steve wiped it on the leg of his jeans and tossed it to me.

Happy to be included in their game, I threw it into the air with no warning to the dog, and Skipper caught it so fast I was startled.

"Incredible!" I said. "No wonder you call him Flash."

"Speed is in his blood. He's from champion retriever stock, but spoiled rotten since he's been with me. All he gets to retrieve for me are balls."

"You don't hunt?"

"Nah. I find no pleasure in it."

I smiled. "But you chose a retriever."

"It just happened. His first owner was a bastard who kept the dog isolated, thinking human contact would ruin him for hunting. It's a common and very stupid belief. Dogs are social by nature and can't live like that, especially Chesapeakes, so I offered a price for the dog the owner couldn't refuse. Skipper has never left my side since I opened the door of that chicken-wire cage. We bought ourselves a couple of tennis balls on the way home, and another great canine hunter retired from the business."

The warmth that welcomed us as soon as we closed the door of the house felt better than sunshine had ever felt. I let it penetrate all through me until the evil chill of the desolate place was gone.

Steve secured both locks. "It's only a few blocks into town. Do you feel like walking?"

"Do you always walk?"

"These short distances, yeah. If you'd rather drive and meet us there..."

"I'll walk with you."

With Skipper Flash in step ahead of us, Steve told me a little of the town's history, but I wasn't absorbing what he said, nor registering the names of the pioneers he mentioned. I was too distracted and confused to concentrate.

The homes and the green lawns became smaller as we neared the business section of town, but the shade trees were as tall and full as they had been in the more exclusive residential area, and these less-pretentious homes had as many gardens and flowering bushes, perhaps more. Tyrone was a well-manicured town, neat and pleasant.

Along the way, we passed very near the house I knew to be Steve's. He said nothing about it. I wondered if anyone was at home there now. A wife? Would he walk to town to get something to eat if he had a wife? That depended on what he wanted to talk about, I supposed. Most people would have simply gone home and fixed themselves a sandwich.

In the business district of town, we passed a corner drugstore, a hardware store and a small boutique, before Steve stopped at a door under a red neon Café sign. Skipper, who was still carrying the little ball, looked up at us with disappointment. The café was off-limits.

"Go find yourself some company, my lad," Steve said as he took the ball from the dog and tossed it into the air. Skipper leaped for it and caught it easily. Two young boys who were riding their bikes along the curb called the dog by name and the retriever bounded off happily toward them.

Hazel's Café was bright with overhead lights and late-afternoon sunshine streaming through its front windows. Several people seated along the orange-topped counter turned curiously. All were looking at me, not at Steve, but it was Steve they greeted. I figured he must be married, because of the way everybody stared, but it wasn't an appropriate moment to ask.

He motioned me to a booth and slid in across from me. "I hope you're hungry so I don't have to eat alone."

My stomach was still queasy after the frights and the emotional overload. "Coffee will do me fine."

"Some pie, at least? Come on. Hazel's pies have won State Fair championships for the past ten years straight. No other pies in Thistle County can call themselves pies."

"What a recommendation! What's your favorite?"

"Apple."

"Great. Mine, too. A slice of apple pie, then." How appropriate, I thought. Apple pie and this little Midwest town that looked like a Norman Rockwell painting. The whole day was probably a dream—the town, the ghostly house, this café, the mysterious man who sat looking at me as though he expected me to tell him why I was in Tyrone and make sense of it for us both.

"Coffee and apple pie for two," he repeated for the waitress. "And a ham-and-cheese sandwich on the side."

In the ensuing small hush our eyes met across the table. I blinked. The impact of Steve's good looks really hadn't hit me until this moment. The power of his eyes caused feelings of uncertainty and vulnerability to surface in me, and I wasn't pleased that his eyes held that kind of power. Scolding the lingering adolescent in me, I reminded myself that age thirty was too old to fall victim to the spell of sensual male eyes, however blue, however penetrating....

Steve wasn't making it easy. He looked at me as though he was seeing me for the first time. His curious interest was so strong it was causing discomfort for us both. I knew it wasn't deliberate, though, and the disquieting moments passed.

Shaken, I muttered, "Everyone knows you. All these people . . . greeting you."

"It's a small town."

"Yes. Much like the town I grew up in. A duck town. Little towns are like ducks, so calm and unruffled above the surface, but below the surface, there's churning and paddling going on all the time."

Steve laughed. "Don't forget the quacking. There's plenty of that, too. And some ducks, you know, just swim in circles all their lives."

"Does the quacking have anything to do with why you missed lunch today?"

"Yep. I got tied up with business. It doesn't happen often."

Our coffee came. Pouring in milk, I asked, "What work are you in?"

"I guess you'd label it public service. I'm the mayor of ducktown."

I nearly spilled my coffee. "You're the mayor? Of Tyrone?"

"I didn't expect it to surprise you that much."

"Well . . . you're rather . . . young. And wearing boots and jeans. Mayors of prairie towns have to have white hair and smell of cigars, don't they?"

He grinned. "And tourists from California have to have pink-framed sunglasses and Mickey Mouse T-shirts, don't they?"

I sipped my coffee and smiled, conceding.

He asked, "Where is your hometown?"

"Montana. A place called Milbury. You wouldn't have heard of it."

He rotated his cup thoughtfully. "Karen, I imagine a lot of people find old photographs in family albums. Something must have spurred you to seek out that house. What was it?"

"The snapshot wasn't in an album. It was sealed in an envelope in a box in the attic."

"You knew that house! I watched you when you were inside. But how the hell could you ever have been there when the place has been boarded up for thirty years?"

"Thirty?"

"Well, as long as I can remember, and I'm thirty-three. And if you didn't know anything about it, why were you shaking? What were you so scared of in there?"

I shifted my eyes from him, then back. "I watched you in there, too. You don't seem to like that house...."

"You're evading my questions."

"Only temporarily. Please, Steve, if you'll talk to me about the house, I promise I'll answer your questions. I have a reason for asking."

He exhaled slowly. "I know you do. Okay. There's something sinister about it. It has always sat there like a big dead monster."

Dead things decay, I thought. That house was decaying too, but slowly, so slowly. "Why does your grandmother keep it? Why doesn't she sell it?"

"No one would buy it."

"Because it's haunted?"

"Partly, yes. Ghosts aren't popular in this town."

"Really?"

"Really."

His sandwich came, and the two slices of pie, slices so large I couldn't help but wonder if the mayor of Tyrone got special attention wherever he went. He took a huge bite and sat back chewing happily, reluctantly postponing the questions he wanted to ask me until I was at ease enough to answer. He tolerated my barrage of questions instead.

"How long ago was it lived in?"

"I told you, I don't remember people ever living there, and I was born in Tyrone."

"It's called the Saxon house. I checked courthouse files and found the record of your grandmother purchasing it at a public auction. The former owner was Wayne Saxon, right?"

"I see you've been busy today."

"Steve, it seems so strange that your grandmother would buy it and then keep it boarded and empty year after year. Why would she?"

"Beats me. She has to pay taxes on it, too. I once tried to talk her into giving it to the town to convert to a convalescent home, but Daphne refuses to discuss anything about that place. She's always said she had her reasons. I think her reasons are nothing more than stubbornness. My grandmother is an impossible woman to figure out. She's eccentric, what can I say? Usually a shrewd businesswoman, but not where the Saxon house is concerned."

"Do you know anything about the people named Saxon?"

"There was some scandal surrounding them, but it was so long ago no one speaks of it nowadays, and certainly Daphne never has."

"What kind of scandal?"

"Something about a murder."

"A murder? And no one speaks of it?"

I watched Steve lose himself in the enjoyment of the man-size sandwich of homemade bread and meat an inch thick. He was a large man, larger than I'd realized at first, and his appetite matched his size.

"I don't think there was ever a murder, or I'd know about it," he said between bites. "You know how stories get started and fill up with air—like balloons getting bigger and bigger. If there really had been a murder, people would still be talking about it. They don't. Nobody talks about it except kids—when the subject of that house comes up and the ghost stories start. Ghosts and murder. Kids' stories.''

''Hasn't your grandmother ever explained why she wanted to own it?''

''She owns half the town. My guess is she just grabbed it up at a giveaway price and then never could unload it.'' He pushed his plate farther from him. ''The question in my mind is more baffling, Karen. What connection did your mother have with that house? Friends of hers lived there, maybe, or relatives?''

''I don't know.''

''You were scared to death of something.''

''Yes, I was....'' In the awkward pause that followed, while I was trying to decide how much I dared tell him, we were interrupted by a heavyset man who appeared in the café doorway, paused when he saw us, and charged at our booth like a water buffalo.

''Hey, cuz! What's going on? I was at your office an hour ago for the meeting with Billy and Barney White.''

''Hell,'' Steve muttered, brushing his napkin over his mouth. ''I forgot about it.''

''So did the Whites evidently. I was the only one who showed up. And after Barney insisted it had to be this afternoon.''

''Lousy time for any meeting,'' Steve muttered. ''Karen Barnett, this is Glen Hadsell.''

''Cousin Glen,'' the man corrected, reaching out his hand to shake mine. ''Steve and me are second cousins. I just heard that cuz was over here at Hazel's preoccupied with a really pretty blonde. No exaggeration there!

Yeah, no wonder you didn't make the meeting, cuz. I'm pleased to meet you, Karen Barnett.''

Steve grinned at his cousin good-naturedly. "Are you sure the meeting with the White brothers was this afternoon?"

"I swear. Oh, you think I just horned in here so I could meet this lovely lady—that's what you're thinking, right? Well, hell yes, I did!" A huge smile cracked his round rugged face. He leaned toward me and lowered his voice. "Keep an eye on this fella, Karen."

"Knock it off, Glen," Steve said mildly.

Glen Hadsell winked at me. "Every woman in this town," he whispered, "keeps an eye on this fella."

I glanced past him to Steve, who was taking all this in stride, without embarrassment, as if such talk was common here. I was, of course, already suspecting I might be wrong about the wife part. Or maybe not....

"What brings you to Tyrone?" Glen Hadsell asked me.

Steve didn't give me a chance to answer. "Cousin, I don't want to be rude, but Karen and I are in the middle of an important conversation."

From his tone, patient but firm, I deduced he knew this interruption would be a long one if he didn't end it.

The man straightened. "Uh-huh! Hmm. Carry on then, cuz. Never mind our scheduled meeting. When the Whites get here I'll explain you're tied up with a personal matter."

"Good. Thanks."

Steve motioned for a coffee warm-up and reached for his pie. I took a bite of the best apple pie I'd ever had in my life and waited for the waitress to disappear again before I said, "Either I've happened upon this town's most eligible bachelor or its most disreputable rogue. Which is it?"

He laughed. "A few of the gentry might credit me with both titles."

"And would they be accurate?"

"No."

He fell into unexpected silence. I waited a long time before he continued reluctantly, "In a place like this a guy who isn't married is, well, watched."

"I see."

I saw very clearly. A man who looked like Steve Hayes and was unmarried—such a man's activities were evidently so closely monitored that his presence in the local café with a strange young woman was all over town in minutes.

He asked, "Why are you smiling? It isn't funny."

I couldn't help laughing. "And, uh, the disreputable-rogue title? Deserved?"

"No way."

I didn't entirely believe him because sometimes I have a problem trusting what handsome men say. But his straightforward, unflinching manner impressed me. I sipped my coffee, grateful the conversation had been diverted to him, hoping he had forgotten the last question he asked before Cousin Glen had barged in.

I asked pleasantly. "Why do I believe you?"

"Because you aren't afraid of men."

"How do you know I'm not?"

"Maybe afraid is the wrong word. You aren't...in awe of men."

I sputtered, "Is anyone?" before I realized how awful that sounded.

It made him laugh.

"I didn't mean it like that," I apologized.

"Sure you did. And it's good, Karen. Puts me at ease."

I wondered whether or not he realized how much he was revealing about himself. Any tuned-in woman could have easily read the implication: he was hotly pursued by women who tried to impress him, and he was sick of it.

I asked, to keep the conversation centered on him, "Are you in awe of women?"

"Yes."

"What? You are?"

"Absolutely. I don't understand women. Maybe we've got the wrong word again. Maybe afraid is more accurate."

"You're not afraid of anybody," I said.

He looked me squarely in the eye. This last statement was true and we both knew it. And he, even out of politeness, wouldn't deny it. I had to ask myself why I *wasn't* the least afraid of this stranger. There was something about him that bothered me, something shadowy, something unsaid. Something I suspected made other people back off from time to time in fear. But what it was, I couldn't define. I could sense it but not react to it.

An awkward silence came between us, but he didn't allow it to linger. That other matter was stubbornly occupying his mind. "Karen, surely you don't expect me to believe that you drove halfway across the country just to look at a house your mother kept a picture of. I'm the guy who was with you inside that house, watching the terror in your eyes. When I took your hand on the stairs, it was ice cold."

"The house..." My voice cracked. I had never talked about my private nightmares to anybody, not even my parents. My automatic defense kicked in, that interior warning that had always caused me to pull back. But now, this moment, sitting in a town in the middle of the prairie in this homey café, I felt the need to unburden myself. Fear was a lonely emotion. I was terribly afraid of that house and I didn't want to be afraid alone. Quite suddenly I was overcome by an urge to tell this man, this stranger, what I had never told anyone.

It was weird, my response to his voice and his eyes. As if he were not a stranger, as if the two of us had sat here and talked before and I knew him and it was all right.

Through the strain of my silence, he finally asked, "Had you heard the house was haunted?"

"I hadn't, no. But it is haunted. There's something in there. Perverse, wrong. I could sense it so strongly."

"I know."

I leaned forward. "What's in there? What is it?"

"I was hoping you could tell *me*."

I sighed and sat back. The plastic of the booth felt cold against my shoulders. I began slowly, "I dreamed about that house long before I ever saw the photograph of it. So then, when I found the picture, after my father died and my mother had been dead many years, I was really curious. I didn't see how I could have dreamed about a house all my life that I'd never seen."

His brow wrinkled. "All your life?"

"Since I was a kid. Ever since I can remember."

"What kind of dreams?"

"Nightmares."

He waited patiently for me to continue. I didn't want to continue, and he sensed it.

"Not nightmares about ghosts, I hope."

"No. I don't know...but the inside looked the way I dreamed it—that's what I had to find out. And I was shocked to see it's the same!"

"The cold burned room off the kitchen—was that room in your dreams?"

"No. In the dream I always saw the carved stairwell and the blue dormer room on the third floor. I clearly saw the outside of the house, too, and the trees in front. But how could I have seen them? How could I?" Remembering, I shuddered.

"Let me compute this, Karen. You saw the house in your dreams and then years later you found the picture, and so you sought out the house and found everything exactly as you dreamed it?" He seemed to think a moment, then glanced up at me in puzzlement. "How can that be?"

I shrugged. "I only know the terror I felt when I pulled out the picture was indescribable. There's something very, very strange...something wrong here."

I touched his arm. "Do people in Tyrone ever talk about anything that happened in the Saxon house? Those murder stories?"

His eyes darkened. "I haven't heard those stories for years. I don't know any details and never thought much about it one way or the other because whenever a house is abandoned, it's always said to be haunted. Every haunted house has to have a murder, right? Isn't there some rule about that? I did ask my grandmother about it once years ago, and she told me the stories were all nonsense, which I'm sure they are. You know how myths surround empty houses."

"Does your grandmother ever go inside?"

"Never that I know of."

"She isn't friendly, is she? She wasn't at all friendly to me on the phone."

Steve had almost forgotten his pie. Now he remembered to take a bite. "Daphne is 'friendly' to only a few."

"Then you don't think it's any use trying to talk to her? I'd like to ask her about it, Steve. About the people who lived there."

"She wouldn't discuss it with a stranger if she won't discuss it with me. But if you want, I'll see what I can find out about the history of the house."

"What about older people? Are your parents here?"

"My parents aren't living. If they were, they'd be an excellent source of information, because they knew the Saxons. They were neighbors."

"Your parents were neighbors of the Saxons?"

Just before popping a large chunk of apple pie into his mouth, Steve answered, "Oh yeah. They lived in that big white house next door."

Chapter Four

If my cup had been full, I'd have spilled coffee all over the table. I set the mug down with a clunk and locked eyes with the man across from me. "You lived next door?"

"My parents did. I don't remember living there. My father died when I was a baby and sometime after that my mother took me to live in Evensen, a little town east of here. When my mother died in my teens I returned to live with Daphne."

"If your parents knew the Saxons, then surely your grandmother did, too."

"No doubt. Daphne is considered the unofficial town historian because she's lived all her life here. Trouble is, my grandmother never makes much distinction between fact and gossip. She thrives on gossip."

"Except about one subject."

"Right. I'll give it another try, though, Karen."

"You're willing to help me?"

"Sure. You've got me intrigued. If there's a logical explanation, we'll find it. Hell, if there's an illogical explanation, I'll find it. Be assured, lovely lady, I always get what I go after."

"Yes, I'm sure you do." I lowered my voice. There was something in his eyes, a spark of challenge. It drew me to him like a moth to flame. Clearing my throat, I pushed back my growing attraction to him. "Steve, I've explained to you why *I* was so nervous in there today. But you haven't explained why *you* were. You just said the house spooks you. Don't you have any idea why?"

"If you want an honest answer, I feel something in there."

"A ghost?"

"Call it what you want."

"You said you don't believe in ghosts."

"I don't. And since you ask, no, I've never seen a sign of ghost spoor."

"My dream was about death."

His eyes closed. "Great."

"You knew that."

"I guessed it. Whose death?"

"I don't know. A woman's, I think. All I saw was the still white hand of someone who'd died, and there were screams, terrible screams all around me. The hand was on the lower landing of the stairs."

"The stairs you damn near fell down."

"I probably would have if you hadn't caught me. When we were there, I could hear and see the whole dream. It was awful!"

"Who was screaming?"

"I think I was. No, someone else was, too. I wasn't alone on the stairs. I could sense the presence of people above me and people below me, but if I saw them in the dream, I don't remember now. I've tried hard to put it out of my mind."

He rubbed his chin. "Why could you see only a hand and not a body?"

"The angle of the stairs. I was above, on the steps looking down."

"Karen—"

He was interrupted by two men in jeans who entered the café noisily, greeting friends who were sitting at the counter. Like Glen Hadsell, they didn't stop to chat but made straight for us.

"Just what we need. The White brothers," Steve said, under his breath. I had already guessed as much.

"Mr. Mayor," one of them said with a broad smile. "Is Hazel's Café where we were gonna meet?"

"No, it wasn't," Steve said and hurriedly introduced me to the two brothers.

"We saw Glen down the street. He said you was here."

"This is pure harassment," Steve said good-naturedly. "You guys have been hounding me about that rezoning ordinance for two years and you know I'm not going to change my mind about it. What's the urgency? I'm tied up right now."

The men looked at me. One said, "Sorry if we're interrupting, but Steve, we got some papers drawn up for the council."

"I'm not going to present anything to the council on your behalf. We're on opposite sides of this issue."

"You're telling them what to do! They won't go against you."

"They vote as they see fit to vote, Billy."

"You gotta listen! We made some adjustments to the plan."

"Are you still within a quarter mile of the river?"

"Well, yeah, but..."

Steve looked at me apologetically, then answered Billy White, "Then we've got nothing to talk about."

I said, "You're engaged in official business. And since we're finished eating, I'll get out of your way."

Steve picked up the check. "I'm going to walk Karen back to her car. If you still want to talk about this, Glen will be here by the time I get back. But if your project is still that close to the river, you're wasting your breath and my time." He smiled. "Have a piece of pie while I'm gone. Hazel has outdone herself today."

At the cashier, I said, "Steve, please don't bother walking all the way back to Sycamore Street when people are waiting for you here. It's gallant of you, but truly unnecessary."

"Of course I'm walking you back."

"No. It's a lovely walk and I'll enjoy it more without the guilt."

He smiled, conceding. "You're staying in Tyrone, then. Where?"

"The motel."

"Good." He escorted me outside.

I asked, "What did you do before you were mayor?"

"I have a law practice here, such as it is. Both jobs leave me time for fishing, which is the main thing. I'll give you a call tomorrow at the motel."

On the sidewalk, he stopped me as I turned to leave. "Karen, promise me you won't try to go into that house alone. It's dangerous."

His words echoed in my brain all the way down the street. Dangerous? What was he talking about? Dirt and shadows and empty rooms and that awful feeling of something about to happen were spooky, but not dangerous.

What did the mayor of Tyrone know about the house that he hadn't told me?

This was a question to ponder while I walked alone through the little business section and out into the tree-lined streets of the residential section. The sun was low in the sky, but it was not yet the twilight of this long soft day of summer. Darkness wouldn't fall until after nine o'clock.

Along the streets children were playing and skating and riding bicycles. People were gathering in their back yards with neighbors. The smell of barbecues filled the air.

This town made me homesick in a way I'd never felt before. Small things—the fragrance of blooming jasmine, the swish of sprinklers on green lawns, the long shadows that crossed the sidewalk, the sight of a squirrel loping along a garden wall—the sweet comfort of the familiar. I felt at home here.

Anxiety welled up again as I neared the abandoned house on Sycamore Street. It stood deathly silent, guarding its secrets. Why had Steve made a departing point of saying it was dangerous and asking me to promise not to go in?

I don't know what made him think I could get into the house again, anyway, unless I climbed up to the tree house and across the branch to the dormer room. A gibbon ape could have done it easily enough, or an agile kid, but I wasn't about to try. As I looked up at the house from my car at the curb, I couldn't get hold of my emotions at all. An evil house. And yet some part of me ached to go back inside. I had missed something in there. I must have!

Another part of me ached to run as far as I could, away from that ghost-infested building, away from this town. Away from that man with the blue, blue eyes and the mysterious smile, and the something...the something that bothered me beyond words. What the devil was it?

I'd been drawn to him like a fly to flypaper and I didn't like that. Was I slipping and falling under the spell of masculine charm? Me? The skeptic who swore it wouldn't happen again?

Well, all right, I was human. But this was different from anything I had experienced. That unidentifiable something about Steve Hayes left me with strong, mixed-together feelings of trepidation and fascination. And strangely, I felt comfort with him where discomfort should have been.

In a half daze, I drove back to the motel, trying to convince myself I'd done the right thing confiding in Steve. Great choice. I'd picked the town's most visible citizen to confide in. Was telling the mayor the same thing as telling the whole town? I didn't know, because I didn't know Steve Hayes. I'd gone on instinct. No, something more than instinct. I'd been affected by that quality about him that bothered—and fascinated—me so much.

My evening was spent with as many thoughts of him as of the Saxon house. I sat in the motel garden in the twilight, trying to work on a jewelry design, which was a stupid idea, because I couldn't concentrate. Sometimes when my mind was full of other things, ideas for designs would come to me suddenly and wonderfully, but this wasn't one of those times.

My jewelry designs were handcrafted by a gold-and-silver smith who was now in my employ full time. Rarely did I work on specific commission, but I had accepted a commission from a manufacturer of leather goods to design three clasps for a line of expensive handbags. I planned to complete the sketches during my trip. Tonight, though, every sketch I tried looked like a cursed ghost, and I finally gave up and read a novel, the hero's face becoming the face of the mayor of Tyrone.

THE SHERIFF'S OFFICE was easy to locate in a building across the street from the courthouse. Two uniformed men sat inside, talking and smoking, one at a wide desk, the other in a chair with his feet up. When I entered, the younger man quickly removed his feet from the desktop and both men stood. Cigarette smoke hung in the stale air.

"Yes, ma'am?" one said. "How can we help you?"

I offered my friendliest smile. "I'm looking for some information. There's an empty house on Sycamore. I believe it's sometimes referred to as the Saxon house. I wondered if you could tell me anything about the people who last occupied that house."

My request stunned them, it seemed, and I was met with silence. The younger man looked at the older, whose eyes darkened with a look I won't ever forget—a look that told me I had hit a sensitive nerve, or at the very least, an unwelcome subject. He cocked his head, frowning, and held out his hand.

"I'm Sheriff Dyer. This here is Deputy Eckles."

The deputy, who also shook my hand, was not frowning, but he did look confused. The expression on the sheriff's face seemed to puzzle him as much as my unexpected inquiry.

"My name is Karen Barnett," I offered. "I'm from California."

"What's your interest in the old Saxon place?" the sheriff asked.

"I'm interested in abandoned houses," I said, returning to the lie, because the truth was unacceptable, impossible. "There are always interesting stories behind long-abandoned homes, especially large beautiful homes like this one."

"A writer, are you? Where would a writer in California hear about a house in Tyrone, Nebraska?"

"I happened onto an old photograph. I've heard the house is haunted."

He smiled, regaining his composure. "Kids say it's haunted."

"What do you say?"

Smoke from the sheriff's cigarette broke in the air—the impact of his hearty laugh. "Me? Ghosts? Ghosts are for kids. Now what I can do for you, ma'am, is supply you with the name of the present owner, if you want information on the house."

"I know Daphne Hayes owns it. I tried to talk to her, but with no luck, so I thought I'd try here. I heard rumors that there was once a murder in the house. Do you know anything about a murder? Is there anything in the police files?"

"Hey," the deputy said. "I've heard that rumor myself."

The sheriff was a man in his sixties, old enough to remember events of thirty or forty years ago, if his residence in Tyrone went back that far. I was hoping it did.

He rubbed his chin thoughtfully and smiled. "The building has been vacant so long I'm surprised there ain't more stories about it than there are. But that's all they are—just stories."

"There's never been a murder in that house?"

The law officer kept smiling and sucking on his cigarette. "I'd know about a thing like murder, now, I would. I been with this sheriff's department for near on forty years and I'd remember a murder."

"Do you remember the family—the Saxons?"

"Sure. Wayne Saxon ran a shop in town. Sporting goods." The sheriff looked at his deputy. "You'd be too young to remember him."

Ervin Eckles scratched the back of his neck. "I don't remember anybody ever living in that house."

Sheriff Dyer crushed out the stub of his cigarette, lifted a package from his pocket—the pocket opposite the large silver badge—and offered me one. I shook my head. He drew out a cigarette, lighted it and took a long drag, blowing more smoke out into the room.

"Did the Saxons move away?" I asked, nearly choking on the smoke and trying not to show my impatience at the way they kept sidetracking my questions.

"They must have been gone when Mrs. Hayes bought the place, because as I recall she bought it at a public auction."

"The Saxons left town, then?"

"Can't say for sure. It was a long time ago."

"Did they ever live in any other house in Tyrone?"

"Not that I know of."

"Then they must have left town."

"Must have."

I felt I was getting the runaround. The sheriff's memory was unbelievably bad. I myself, having been raised in a small town where everybody's business was everybody else's, found it hard to believe that Sheriff Dyer had such little knowledge of the family named Saxon. I supposed if he didn't personally know them, he would have no reason to remember. Or to know why they left or where they went. Yet Wayne Saxon owned a business here and a very large home. The sheriff must know something more about him. Maybe he just felt it was no business of a stranger, an outsider.

I persisted, anyway, steering to areas he would have to know about. "What happened to the shop?"

"Closed down. There's been a liquor store in that location for a good many years now."

I pushed back a lock of hair from my forehead; the day was getting warm and there was no air-conditioning in the sheriff's office, only a slow-revolving ceiling fan that churned the smoke around. "Would it be possible for me to check police files to see if any crime was ever committed in that house?"

The sheriff looked at me suspiciously, with growing hostility. I was afraid I'd made an enemy of him by blatantly doubting his memory. Several awkward seconds passed before he answered, "Sure. Though I can assure you, miss, my memory ain't faltering yet. Ask my deputy here. Anything that's gone on in this town this half of the century, I remember."

"I certainly didn't intend to imply that your memory was faltering, Sheriff Dyer. I'm merely scratching for a story, any kind of story, even an insignificant one."

"Yeah, I know writers are persistent." He rubbed his chin. "We'll check the records, if it'll please you. Them homes on Sycamore was all built between 1930 and '37. We'll go back to the thirties files."

"Files that old will be in the basement," the deputy said. "Want me to take care of it?"

"Nah." The sheriff stretched out his right leg and flexed the knee a time or two. "Them stairs is good for the old knee. Need the exercise."

"I hope it isn't a great deal of trouble," I said.

"No trouble. Won't take no time at all."

I didn't like the way the sheriff wouldn't meet my eyes. From the instant I'd mentioned the Saxon house, he had acted strangely; I was sure I wasn't imagining it. I wasn't imagining his curiosity about me, either. Someone from California popping up, asking a lot of questions. I couldn't blame him for being curious.

He led me down a set of stairs to a stale dark storage room, where he switched on the overhead light—a single bare bulb—and began searching through files stacked along a back wall. "You said you happened on a picture? From someone who knew this Saxon family or what?"

"I had no information about the house at all when I drove in here, except the name of the town. Mayor Hayes told me about the Saxon family."

For a fraction of a second the sheriff looked as if he'd been shot; Steve's name hit him like a bullet between the eyes. He tried his best, I could tell, to cover his shock at hearing the name come whizzing out of my mouth, but his reaction had already been noted; nothing he could do now would change it. His own shock reverberated back to mine. Why on earth would Steve's name trigger such a reaction?

"Mayor Hayes," the man repeated. "Are you a friend of our mayor's?"

"I met him only today quite by accident. I was looking at the empty house when he happened to be...near there, and he saw me and stopped."

"There ain't nothing here," he muttered, pushing at the file folders. "Look for yourself if you want. Of course, I could've told you that. But I'll keep looking. I'm up to the early sixties."

I'd been closely watching him go through the crime files. They were very thin files. The city records were filed separately from the county, and the sheriff was right, it didn't take long to go through them. The only murder he pulled up out of there was that of a transient, committed—as nearly as the law officers could determine—by another transient, who sped away on the next train and probably was never found.

Dyer closed the files. "I assume then," the sheriff said as we started up the steps, "that it was Mayor Hayes who told you this cock-and-bull murder story."

"Yes."

"He don't believe such a story, does he?"

"I don't think so. It was just conversation."

"He didn't ask you to check it out?"

"Oh, no. This was my idea. But he's promised to find out what he can about the house—hopefully from his grandmother."

"Hmm. He'll need some luck there. I take it you ain't been inside."

"Yes, I have. Mayor Hayes has a key. He was kind enough to take me in."

A strange noise rose from the sheriff's throat. "Steve was inside that house?"

I drew back as the increasing unease began to consume me. There was something very wrong with this conversation.

Back in his office upstairs, the sheriff turned to his deputy, who was pinning up a new picture on the Wanted Criminals bulletin board. "Did you ever believe any of them ghost stories, Erv?"

He pushed in the thumbtack and took another out of his mouth. "When we were young, us kids wouldn't go in that empty house on a triple dare. No, sir, we wouldn't." He turned around. "We used to look at the windows at night thinking we might see the ghost everybody talked about."

Dyer chuckled. "And did you ever see it?"

"Oh, yeah. Once we did. At least we convinced ourselves we did. There was a light moving around in the high window, under the gables there, and the ghost of a woman. That's what we saw."

"No wonder them old stories never died down. You kids always kept them going. Well, I reckon that's normally the way ghost stories spread. Kids and their wild imaginations."

I asked, "Have you any idea what prompted the Saxons to just . . . leave?"

Both men looked at each other and the sheriff shrugged. "It was a darn long time ago, Miss Barnett."

I felt my welcome wearing thin because I was repeating questions to see if I'd keep getting the same answers. I couldn't help myself. I knew the sheriff remembered; he just didn't want to tell me.

Another thing was goading me—the question about Steve—and it took more than a little courage to bring it up. Swallowing hard, I asked, "Sheriff, why did you seem so surprised to hear that Mayor Hayes had taken me inside the house?"

He hesitated. A look that chilled me crossed his eyes. His voice was strained when he spoke. "The mayor evidently doesn't realize how dangerous it is in a house that's deteriorated through a lot of years of sitting empty, especially a house that's been partly burned."

It was a stupid response to my question and we both knew it. I said, "He would know the condition of the house, since the property is in his family."

Dyer looked at me, almost through me. "Yeah, maybe."

It was becoming evident to me that Steve Hayes wasn't the only person in Tyrone who never ventured inside the old house on Sycamore Street. Nobody did. Except the alleged ghost. Something had driven the people out, and the house had been abandoned by everything but evil.

"When was the fire?" I asked as an afterthought, on my way out.

"Before it was sold, as I recall. Brought down the price considerably. I don't know why Mrs. Hayes never restored the house. I guess it'd be a waste of money without a buyer."

"Then why would she buy it?"

"Beats me. It's her hobby, though, buying property."

I felt drained when I left the sheriff's office. Checking the old crime files had proved futile, and the sheriff had volunteered all but nothing. His shifting eyes and startled reactions to my questions had told me more than he had, so all I'd really learned was that there was something he didn't want me to know. Was the mayor hiding something, too?

There were obviously a lot of things I didn't know about this strange little town of Tyrone. That summer morning as I walked out of the sheriff's office and into bright sunshine, I had no idea what horror I was getting myself into by staying and trying to find out.

Chapter Five

I knew the evil was real. There wasn't much else I knew about what was going on, but I knew there was evil around me. I had seen it through the lens of a dream, and I had felt it in the echoing heartbeats of that house. And I had sensed it in the sheriff's office. I knew the evil was real, and I knew evil was what repelled Steve and me in the half-burned-out room in the far back wing of the Saxon house.

What I didn't know was what the evil had to do with me, or why it had "called" me. One way or another, I had to find out. I had the growing conviction that if I didn't, it would consume me. And maybe others.

Frustrated because my determination had no plan nor direction, I cut across the tree-lined street toward an old redbrick building with a stone-carved plaque over the door that said Tyrone City Library, 1929.

I entered a large room where the smell of books and ink and cigar smoke had been long assimilated into the walls and carpet. The young woman who sat behind the long low desk was blond, in her early twenties, and she wore bright pink plastic earrings that hung nearly to her shoulders. Her blouse was cut so low in front that at least half an inch of her lace bra protruded above it. Her glossy red smile was friendly. The placard on her desk said, Kimberly Johnstone, librarian, and she looked less like a librarian than any woman I'd seen yet in this conservative little town.

"I'm looking for information on the history of Tyrone," I said.

The idea of passing myself off as a writer, for lack of an alternative, kept surfacing. By now the idea was taking on the earmarks of a plan. I wouldn't push the lie, but I might be forced to fall back on it.

"The best book we have is *The History of Thistle County.* Tyrone, of course, is the county seat. All our history books are on the shelf just under the window." The scent of flowery perfume rose as the pretty young librarian pointed in the direction of the shelves by the window.

I thanked her and set about looking through the books, with no idea what on earth I was looking for. The library was very quiet; apart from the librarian I was the only person there. Presently I looked up from the table. "One book ends in 1943 and the other in 1936. Have you anything more recent? Anything about the townspeople? High-school yearbooks, even?"

"Yearbooks would be over at the high-school library. What are you specifically looking for? Maybe I can help."

"I'm trying to learn what I can about a certain house in Tyrone—the empty Victorian-style house on Sycamore."

I half expected some startled reaction like I'd gotten from the sheriff, but this young woman smiled with genuine interest. "Oh, that house! Might you be thinking of buying it?"

"Is it for sale?"

"Good heavens, I wouldn't have thought so. But since it's empty, I guess there's a possibility. Though I've never seen a For Sale sign or anything."

"I'm researching old houses," I explained, hating the lie but getting used to it. It wasn't entirely a lie anyhow, I rationalized; I was researching one particular old house. I said, "I've heard it's supposed to be haunted."

"I've heard that, too. Mrs. Wycoff, a lady I used to baby-sit for, told me once she actually saw a ghost in a window, but I didn't know whether to believe it or not. I'm not overly superstitious about ghosts and that sort of thing."

I smiled. "Neither am I. Somebody told me there was once a murder in the house and the ghost is the murder victim."

"Kids used to say so. They said the ghost was a girl. I haven't heard any talk of it for quite a long time."

"Do you know the owner? Mrs. Hayes?"

"Not very well. I've talked to her here in the library." Kimberly Johnstone lowered her voice. "Mrs. Hayes is in her seventies now, but they say she was once the most beautiful woman in this valley. She wears velvet skirts and big lace cuffs, you know, and strings upon strings of real pearls, like those rich old ladies in the movies! In this town she's like a queen. She has wonderful Christmas parties for poor children and things like that. Are you writing a magazine article?"

"I, uh . . . I'm just researching on my own."

I returned the book to the shelf and approached the librarian's desk. Kimberly pulled a paper cup of iced cola from under the counter and began sipping through the straw while she looked up at me with renewed interest. "You're doing an article on abandoned and haunted houses! How exciting! I've always wanted to do something like that. Writing, I mean.''

I smiled weakly, wishing the truth weren't so complicated. But I had her attention, so I'd make the most of it. I hadn't said I was a reporter, but I could go on sounding like one. "What about Mrs. Hayes's grandson? Do you know him?''

Her eyes widened. Her lips released the straw. Now I had a startled reaction. "Steve? Everybody knows him. He's our mayor.''

"And an attorney, I understand. How long has he been in office?''

"Three ... three and a half years.'' Her smiled had faded. "You're not going to write about our mayor, are you?''

"He'd be a good subject, don't you think?''

"No!''

The protest was so spontaneous and so strong that the young woman, realizing how it sounded, tried to shadow her initial response. She set the cola on the floor by her chair and began to twirl a lock of her hair speculatively. "I mean, knowing Mayor Hayes ... he'd ... he wouldn't like it.''

"Why not?''

"Well, he's a private person.''

So! I thought. More secrets! This was curious. "Most mayors, being in public life, are used to publicity. They rather thrive on it, I should think.''

She wouldn't meet my eyes. "You're in Tyrone, Nebraska. We're off the beaten path.''

"It's an interesting town,'' I responded, pretending I didn't catch the gist of what she was trying to say, which was, of course: Don't ask questions about our mayor.

"Tell me about your mayor." I smiled innocently while I watched her nervously twirl the lock of hair. I wondered if she had some personal connection with the subject of our discussion. Maybe she had some reason of her own to want to discourage any more questions about Steve.

The librarian suddenly busied herself stamping the inside jackets of a stack of books. "I don't know anything about Mayor Hayes."

"Did you vote for him?"

"We all did."

"Who was the man who ran against him?"

"No one ran against him."

"I see," I said. But I did not see. The more I prodded her on the subject of Steve Hayes, the more the librarian hedged.

This was getting as eerie as the house. A mayor who ran unopposed and did not like publicity? A mayor whose name, uttered by an outsider, made everybody nervous? It didn't make sense. All mayors want to publicize their towns. Something wasn't right. Neither the librarian nor the sheriff wanted to discuss their most prominent town official with me—the same town official all the single women watched like swooping hawks, according to Glen Hadsell, because he was the eligible prince of the kingdom. What a weird place I had stumbled into!

This young librarian knew Steve better than she wanted to let on. But she did not know anything about the Saxons; the name was barely familiar to her.

When I emerged from the town library, more confused than when I went in, Skipper Flash was trotting along the street in front of the courthouse by himself. His Honor the Mayor was nowhere in sight. As soon as he noticed me, the dog came bouncing over, tail wagging furiously, carrying something in his mouth. When I leaned over to pet him, he set the little ball on the sidewalk at my feet—the same ball he had found yesterday at the abandoned house. He looked up at me with bright begging eyes.

"Still have your treasure, do you, Skipper? Okay, do your stuff." I picked up the ball and threw it a short distance—toward the building so he wouldn't bound into the street after it.

I needn't have worried. The ball never got close to the ground. Skipper leaped up and caught it in the air with his usual speed and precision and brought it back at once for me to throw again.

"He'd keep that up all day if you were willing," a voice said behind me.

I turned. Steve was standing on the sidewalk in front of the police station. As he fell into step beside me, the adrenaline started pumping through my body. At this point, I didn't understand what was causing it—his good looks, the nearness of him, or the odd reactions of the sheriff and the librarian to the mere mention of his name. He didn't look like a man people would fear. Or did he? I was beginning to wonder if people were indeed afraid of him. And if so, why?

He said, "I just stopped at the sheriff's office to see if there's anything in police records to confirm the rumors of a murder. Chuck said you'd been asking the same thing."

"There isn't a thing on record."

"It would have surprised me if there had been. We don't have murders in Tyrone."

"The sheriff barely remembered the Saxons," I said. "But surely it wouldn't be hard to find someone who does."

"I've been thinking about it. The Saxons left before..."

He stopped abruptly. A man was running across the street yelling his name and something about a liquor-license violation. Steve turned quickly. "Look, Karen. The woman who runs the Pawnee Saloon, Maude O'Grady, is a friend of mine. Maude's lived in Tyrone all her life. Why not talk to her? The saloon is open for lunch and specializes in roast-beef sandwiches. I'll meet you over there as soon as I find out what this latest problem is."

Since I had no idea where the saloon was, I walked along the tree-shaded sidewalk for half a block until I reached the intersection of Main Street. From here I could see the far end of the street near the railway depot and a weather-beaten sign that read Pawnee Saloon.

As I walked, I thought of my journey from California across the western states. So many small towns had empty stores and a half-lived-in look. Not so Tyrone. It was as if time had stood still here. There were no new buildings that I could see, but all of the old ones were well maintained and in use. Even taking my time, looking in the store windows, my walk the length of Main Street took only six or seven minutes.

The interior of the Pawnee Saloon was quite dark to someone coming in from the bright sun's glare. I entered what could almost have been a movie set—a Western saloon with mirrors behind an enormous bar, old carved-wood and brass fixtures, and round tables down the center. The establishment might well have sat on this corner since before the turn of the century, looking then just as it did today.

At a few minutes before noon on a summer day, there were only two customers, both men, sitting at the bar. I took a seat at one of the tables, and a smiling waitress approached at once.

"Hot day, isn't it?" she said.

"It feels good in here, though, with the fans."

"What'll you have?"

I was gazing at the displays of guns and tomahawks, and bows and arrows that covered the walls. Ordering an ice tea or diet cola didn't seem appropriate, even for a tourist wandering in, so I asked for a tap beer, knowing I probably wouldn't drink half of it. A beer in early afternoon was decadent for me. I ordered the recommended roast-beef sandwich with it.

When the waitress, a dark-haired young woman in her early twenties, brought the ice-cold beer, she lingered as though she wanted to alleviate some of the boredom of her job by visiting. I was glad for the opening; I could bring up my obsession once again. I smiled at her. "I hear there's a huge house in this town that's so haunted no one has lived in it for decades. Is it true?"

"Oh, yes! Have you seen it?"

"Yes. It's a beautiful old house."

"I know!" When the girl leaned in close to me, coins jingled in the white pocketed apron she wore over her jeans. "A woman was murdered in that house."

A chill went up the back of my neck. "Who was she?"

"A woman who lived there, I've heard. It's her ghost, and she comes out nights and walks around the house. People have seen her at the upper window."

"Who is supposed to have killed her?"

"Her husband, I think."

"What happened to him?"

"He was probably hanged or something."

Every town had its myths and fables, I thought. No point in mentioning the fact that there was no evidence whatsoever to support this claim. "I was told your manager here at the Pawnee Saloon might remember the last occupants of that house. Is there a Maude O'Grady here?"

The girl brightened. "Sure. Maude's my great aunt. I'll go get her. It'll just take a second."

She disappeared through a door behind the bar and came out a few minutes later with a plump elderly woman wearing tan slacks and a sleeveless overblouse. Her hair had been dyed an uneven shade of red, and she wore earrings made from real Indian arrowheads.

Maude O'Grady extended a friendly hand, shook mine hard and sat down beside me at the table. No other customers had come in and the two men at the bar seemed involved in deep discussion. Ceiling fans whirred above.

"Cecilia tells me you're a tourist," she said.

"Yes. My name is Karen Barnett. I was asking her about the haunted house on Sycamore Street."

Mrs. O'Grady laughed. "I couldn't personally say if it is or isn't haunted. I only know it's been empty for the past quarter of a century and nobody wants to buy it."

Cecilia chimed in enthusiastically. "*Buy* it? Nobody will even go *in* there!"

Maude glanced at her exuberant niece with disapproval. "Nobody can go in there. It's private property."

"What I was wondering," I said as casually as I could, "is whether you remember the last occupants of the house—the Saxon family."

Immediately I detected suspicion in Maude's eyes.

"That would be the woman who was murdered," Cecilia said.

Her aunt frowned. "What is this talk of murder, Cecilia? Don't be silly." She turned to me. "We've never had a murder in our little town. I'm not bragging, mind you, I'm complaining. It only proves what an unimaginative lot we are. Good pioneer stock inhabit this valley. Boring as dry straw, but good people, except for the young fools who feel cheated and invent murder stories to make up for the lack of excitement. Sure, I knew the Saxons—slightly. They lived here, good heavens, it must have been twenty-five or thirty years ago."

"Do you know why they left, and why their house was sold at public auction?"

Cecilia cut in once again. "Because she died, and he killed her."

Maude's impatience took the form of a withering glance. "Cecilia, there are some vegetables to slice in the kitchen. Get on back there and justify your existence."

"Come on, Aunt Maude! I want to hear more about this."

"There's nothing to hear. We're talking about facts here, not *Halloween Three*." Mrs. O'Grady turned to me. "We've created a generation of kids who watch horror movies until they develop unnatural twitches and a thirst for blood. It's criminal the way kids are nowadays. What was it you asked?"

"I asked if you knew why the Saxons moved."

"I can't rightly say I recall."

"You don't know if the house sale had to do with... with Mrs. Saxon's death?"

The eyes that squinted at me were scrutinizing. "Who steered you here and told you I might have known that Saxon family?"

"Your mayor. Steve Hayes."

The plump body stiffened like a puppet whose every wire had just been tightened.

That startled reaction to his name again!

"Steve Hayes?" she repeated with a small squeak. "You talked to Mayor Hayes about the Saxon house?"

A now familiar foreboding, a sense of something terribly wrong, passed through me once again. I pretended not to notice the sudden change in Maude O'Grady that had moved in like a thunderstorm. "I was looking at that house when he happened by on his way into town. He told me his grandmother is the present owner, and when I asked about the previous occupants, he suggested you might remember them."

Maude grinned mischievously, almost viciously. "You couldn't ask Her Royal Highness. I expect Her Royal Highness wouldn't talk to strangers."

Steve picked that moment to show up at the saloon. His tall form filled the entire doorway as he paused there with the sun at his back. He let the door swing shut and came in, greeting Maude and her grandniece as he approached our table, pulled up a chair and sat down.

"Were you able to supply Karen with any information?" he asked the proprietor.

"What do you mean?" Maude answered, pulling nervously at one of her arrowhead earrings.

Trying to sound as casual as possible to conceal the fact that I was picking up very uncomfortable vibrations from Maude O'Grady, I volunteered, "No one seems to know why the Saxons left Tyrone. There's a possibility Mrs. Saxon died."

Cecilia, who had no intention of leaving for the kitchen as her aunt had demanded, was fidgeting in her chair, refusing to look at the older woman and bubbling with interest at the subjects of murder and ghosts.

"Steve," Cecilia said, "people have seen a ghost in that house, and you know it. Everybody says it's her—Mrs. Saxon. You've heard that, I know you have."

"I've heard a lot of different rumors," he answered. "They don't mean much, Cecilia."

"It was the husband—"

"Cecilia Ann, will you let that nonsense rest!" her aunt demanded.

The girl ignored the command once again. "There's evidence of the ghost!"

"What evidence?" Steve asked.

"You know perfectly well! Several people have seen a ghost in the upstairs window, and wandering around the grounds."

"I've been inside the house several times and never saw anything." He turned his charismatic smile on her. "It's just a decaying old building."

He was playing down, or rather covering, his true feelings about that house, feelings he had willingly confided to me. Yet I was a stranger to him and this girl was not. Perhaps it was *because* I was a stranger that he allowed himself to express his true feelings.

I realized he was protecting the house—protecting a house he admittedly hated! Evidently he was eager to keep stories down. That might matter to his grandmother if she ever wanted to sell the property, but it puzzled me why it should matter here in this saloon with Maude O'Grady and her grandniece.

Cecilia's thoughts were mine. "Then why doesn't anybody know why those people left?" she asked. "Did you ever ask your grandmother?"

"I can't recall," Steve answered.

"Nobody remembers? That makes no sense!"

Cecilia's perseverance was making her aunt nervous. I watched Maude very closely. She would glance at Steve and her jaw would jut out like a bulldog's.

"You're right," he said. "It doesn't."

"We knew them," Maude conceded defensively. "I used to see Mary Saxon at the beauty shop. Nice lady, she was, but quiet. Young and pretty. Sometimes she worked in the sporting-goods shop, helping him. They were private people, not interested in the social goings-on, even though they lived in the ritzy part of town. The store failed, as I recall."

Steve scratched his chin thoughtfully, a habit of his I was getting used to. "If the business failed, it would have been public knowledge. So would an untimely death."

"We're talking about thirty years ago, maybe more."

He answered mildly, "You're known for your crackerjack memory, Maude."

She laughed heartily as she lifted her large body clumsily from the chair. "You're overestimating me, kid. Though, mind, I love you for it. I've always loved you for the way you can get on the good side of people. Karen, I guess you're looking for a good ghost story to take home with you. There ain't one here that has any facts behind it, I'm afraid. Wish there was. Hell, I like a good ghost story as much as the next guy. Even a juicy scandal would be nice. Dull town, this. Nothing ever happens in Tyrone."

I smiled. "Maybe I can find someone who claims to have seen the ghost."

"Right!" Cecilia boomed. "There must be a dozen at least—"

Her aunt tugged at her arm, not gently. "How long are you going to sit there jabbering about nothing while your customer waits for her lunch?"

Cecilia drew back. "Oh! Oh, no! Your sandwich! I forgot all about it."

"So did I," I said honestly.

Steve said, "Make it two sandwiches. No, three—I'm hungry. And a beer."

When we were alone at the table, Steve said, "Well, Karen, this is interesting. Mentioning the name Saxon around here is like opening a can of worms."

"Haven't you ever noticed it before?"

"I never thought about it. It never came up."

"People don't talk about your grandmother's empty house?"

"Almost never. It's been there so long I guess they don't think about it."

"Except people like Cecilia who love ghost stories."

He nodded thoughtfully. "People who weren't around thirty years ago..."

When his beer came, he didn't seem very interested in it. "Karen, I spoke with my grandmother last night. She admits she knew that family when they lived next door to her son and daughter-in-law. Her description of them matches Maude's—they were private people. She said it wasn't known why they left hurriedly, other than that they had financial problems. She didn't say anything about Mrs. Saxon's dying." He sipped the beer. "It's damned odd so many people are claiming memory lapses—including Daphne. Thirty years is a long time to you and me, but it isn't long to some of these people. Those, at least, in their sixties and seventies."

"Was it thirty years exactly?"

"Yeah, thirty. According to Daphne."

"Did the house sit empty for five years before your grandmother bought it? I checked public records that give the purchase date as twenty-five years ago."

"That's probably when the deal became final. I suppose it did sit empty. Damned thing is nothing but a burden that ought to be torn down. In fact I'm going to talk to Daphne about tearing it down."

That idea hit me like a jab in the chest. *Tear it down?* The house was beautiful by anyone's standards. Settled back in the trees, behind its stretch of green lawn, it was almost serene. It had been a source of horror for me, though. I didn't know why I should hate the idea of its being destroyed, but the idea made me feel ill.

Maude, not Cecilia, brought our sandwiches. Steve welcomed the food with more gusto than he had the beer. I remembered he was on his lunch hour. My sandwich was so thick I could barely get it into my mouth, but I managed. I hadn't thought I was hungry, but Maude's food was excellent and went down easily. We ate listening to soft strains of country music from a radio somewhere in the saloon.

Steve said, "What the hell happened thirty years ago that nobody wants to talk about?"

"You think people are deliberately covering up something?"

"I have no doubt of it. Have you?"

"No. They all couldn't just . . . forget."

"Of course not."

I lowered my voice even though there was no one to hear. The two men at the bar were still involved in their own conversation, and Maude and Cecilia were nowhere in sight. "Steve, I can understand why people in a community might not open up to someone coming from outside asking questions. But you're the mayor of this town! Why wouldn't they tell you?"

"That's what I'd like to know. After getting nowhere with my grandmother last night, I talked to a couple of people this morning—my doctor and his wife and a re- tired railroad engineer who were in my office. All people in their sixties who should have known the Saxons. They all claim bad memories."

"Damn. What can that house have to do with me?"

"That's the thing that's driving me, Karen. What connection do you have with this? How old are you?"

"Thirty."

"You look younger. Maybe your parents knew the Saxons and talked about them."

"It wouldn't explain my accurate dreams of the inside of the house."

"Dammit, there has to be some way of finding out where these people went, and where they are now."

I gazed at his blue eyes. "Do you remember your grandfather?"

"He died when my dad was in his teens. Daphne has been a widow for forty years."

"Why do you think she was so adamant about not al- lowing me to go in the house? Why did you say there'd be hell to pay if she found out you let me in?"

"Not you particularly, Karen. Anyone. She doesn't like anyone in there."

"Neither does the sheriff."

"What do you mean?"

"When I told him you took me through, he almost swallowed his cigarette. He said you didn't realize the dangers."

"You mean as if you and I were little kids sneaking through an off-limits house? What kind of sense does that make?"

"Not very much."

He pulled the crust off the bread of his second sandwich. "Daphne doesn't know I have a key. I had it made along with other keys to property Daphne owns. In case she comes to her senses one day about leaving it abandoned, I could show it to prospective buyers. Also I'm responsible for taking care of her properties. Someone else needs a full set of keys."

"Sure, but you're kidding! She doesn't even want *you* in there?"

"Absolutely not."

"The sheriff must know that then, because he seemed so surprised. Maybe I shouldn't have said anything...."

Steve laughed. "The sheriff is afraid of my grandmother like everybody else in town. He sometimes forgets he works for me."

Everything seemed so unreal, like an illusion. From time to time I had the sensation of floating above all this and looking down, trying to get far enough out of the mist of fear to gain some kind of objectivity. I touched the arm of the man who sat across from me. "Steve, what is the sheriff guarding? What secrets lie in the dust of that old house?"

His blue eyes riveted on mine so intensely I felt the weight of their power. I'd have given anything to know what he was thinking.

Steve broke the gaze. He reached into his pocket and threw some bills on the table.

"Let's get out of here," he said.

Chapter Six

Walking down Main Street with the mayor of Tyrone was like navigating an obstacle course. Not a person passed without speaking to him, and most wanted to stop to talk. I felt their stares, especially those of the women.

"They wonder who you are," Steve said.

"I wonder who I am, too." I was still caught in the euphoric illusion that none of this was real. "Everything about this town makes me feel strange. Where are we going?"

"Somewhere away from the stares where we can talk."

Steve was skilled at cutting off unwelcome conversations quickly, without offending anyone. Most of them, aware I was the same woman he had been with yesterday at Hazel's Café, were merely curious. His cutting people off now, on the street, implied he was preoccupied with me. Which he was. I felt like an object of scorn for interfering with the way things ought to be.

We reached the municipal building. Steve led the way to the parking lot in the rear where he opened up the door of a late-model blue pickup. Before I could get in, a huge flash of yellow fur leapt up behind, nearly knocking me off my feet.

"Great manners, Skip!" Steve exclaimed, embarrassed. "Just push the lady out of your way!"

The dog sat on the seat of the truck looking at me, his wet tongue hanging out.

"I didn't even see him!" I said. "I had no idea he was behind us."

"He's never far from me. Knows where I am every minute. Here, you old fool, get out of there!"

"It's okay. He doesn't bother me," I insisted. "He wants to go so badly."

"He'll drool on your neck."

I laughed. "It won't be the first time a dog drooled on my neck. I always had a dog when I was a kid, and I adore old Skip. Let him come." I climbed up into the truck beside the big yellow dog and gave him a hug.

"You've won his loyalty. Now you can do no wrong." Steve started the engine. He circled quickly through the small business section and headed down a side road toward a long, winding shadow of tall trees.

"The river," I said.

"Have you seen the river?"

"No, only the trees."

"My favorite places are in the river."

"*In* the river?"

"The Pawnee River is full of small wooded islands and sandbanks, some dense thickets and grassy marshes. Everything a kid could ask for. I spent many of my younger days around this area."

He parked at the side of the road under a shade tree. "I think you'll like it here."

The dog ran ahead, splashing in the shallows, scaring up frogs, as we traversed a sandbar veined by slow-moving water toward a mysterious dark island that lay deep within the wide expanse of the river. The sand was white and pure; in my imagination I could feel it warm and wet between my toes. Birds were abundant in the river, their competitive voices constant. Insects buzzed and hissed. Cool air rose off the water, a relief from the heat of the midday sun.

"This is the most beautiful place I've ever seen!"

"We're heading for my secret spot. I like to think no one ever comes here but me. At least I've never seen signs of another human around here, so maybe no one does."

In the center of the thick copse the water pooled into a mirror-smooth pond that reflected the colors of the sky and the leafy overhang. Lily pads floated at the edge of the pool. We sat on a fallen log.

Steve flicked a pebble into the still water. "Make a wish. Tradition demands it."

"What tradition?"

"Mine."

I didn't want to make a wish, but I thought of one just the same as I sat beside Steve on that mystical summer afternoon, tensely aware of the beauty and the mystery of him.

He leaned his elbows on his knees and gazed at the blue water. "Now the ghosts are far away."

"Why did we come all the way out here?"

"Because I wanted you to see my river. This seemed like where we ought to be."

"Your river?"

"Yep. Mine. Ask anybody in the valley whose river this is."

"I'm glad you wanted to share your river with me. It's so exclusive here, so... cut off from the world."

"Karen, something about you—or everything about you—gets to me. I think you know that. I've been getting the impression it's mutual. Is it?"

Nothing in his behavior thus far had prepared me for such an abrupt burst of honesty, and it threw me. My response was a self-conscious smile, which seemed to be all the answer he needed. He touched my arm gently.

"You need me," he said.

I looked at him quizzically.

"I don't think you can solve this mystery without me."

"I . . . You're right, I can't."

"Karen, think. Is there anything about your dreams you haven't told me?"

I was getting very mixed messages from him right now. He talked, in his way, about attraction, then dropped the topic as if he hadn't brought it up. Maybe . . . maybe he was simply the most honest man I'd ever met. Of course there was attraction between us; there had been from the moment we first saw each other. The dictates of social manners demanded we play around it, not directly acknowledge it. Steve evidently played by different rules. So he was attracted and he knew I was. He acknowledged it verbally. Nothing more. Nothing less. I wondered how many women had been thrown into a tailspin by this obviously very confirmed bachelor who didn't like women to be in awe of him.

"Karen?"

"What?"

"I asked if there's anything about your nightmares you haven't told me."

I gazed at him. "Actually there is. One thing. I didn't dream about just one hand. I saw two, and only one of them belonged to a dead person."

He cringed. "How can that be?"

I grew very thoughtful, trying to find a way to articulate my swirling thoughts. "It's been hard for me to separate the flashes—the images. But the longer I stay in

Tyrone, and the more I'm forced to think about them, the easier it is to make sense of them."

"And?" he asked, leaning closer and flashing those amazing blue eyes over my face.

"All right. This is what I'm getting. The still hand wears a diamond ring. Another hand lifts the ring—steals it—the jewels sparkle when the ring's removed from a limp finger. That's why I knew it wasn't a fall from the stairs that killed...whoever it was. Someone wanted her ring. Steve, isn't it eerie that there would be rumors of murder and no evidence of a murder and yet I think I might have seen a murder? Am I psychic?"

Steve thought a moment and shook his head. "We don't know. It's certainly eerie. What we've got to do is find somebody who will talk about the Saxons so we can make sense of what you're 'seeing.'" He tossed another pebble into the water. "This puzzle is eating at me. Something either is or was in that house, I'm sure. I've always felt something in there. Perhaps we're both psychic, and your ability is stronger."

I felt a chill go down my spine. Certainly I'd had flashes of other things before, but this was the strongest and had lasted a lifetime.

"What I know is that I'm being lied to by my grandmother and the sheriff, and others, and I don't like it. I don't like anything about it!"

He rose from the log and stepped to the sandy shore of the tiny island, where he knelt on one knee and dipped his hand into a channel of shallow running water.

I watched him scoop water into his hands and drink deeply while some of the water spilled over the front of his shirt.

He looked up, wiping his mouth. "Want a drink?"

"Of river water?"

"It's never killed me yet. I go on the theory that the sand cleans it."

I knelt at his side. "Then I trust you."

"Here..." He dipped into the cold water again and offered me a drink from his hands.

I cupped my hands over his while I drank. At the first touch of water to my lips, the world began to spin. Was it an elixir of magic? I grasped his hands more tightly, wondering if the sweetness of the water was the taste of the river or the taste of Steve's skin.

The swirling stopped and everything became utterly still. We were caught in a cone of timelessness while everything around us was frantically, wildly pulsing, and we were untouched by any of it.

The taste of water from Steve's hands was as intoxicating as a witch's potion. Was it the taste of him or the touch of him that affected me so? Or was it the sun reflecting off the water into his eyes? And my eyes? With my hands still cupped around his, I looked up at him and knew that whatever had happened just now hadn't happened only to me. His gaze—curiosity mixed with disbelief—locked with mine. Recognition of something beyond our knowing passed between us.

He whispered, "Karen?"

The whisper came like an echo—from his lips, from the bird songs, from the river.

I couldn't answer. I could only hear the echoes. I could only feel a soothing warmth unlike anything I'd ever experienced. Our gaze held until I bent to sip once again the perfumed water from his hands.

Without drying his hands, he touched my hair, brushing it back from my face so gently I could feel nothing, only see the movement, like the fluttering of a butterfly.

"Karen? Who are you?"

"Who...are *you*?"

The river rippled like music beside us. He leaned forward and pressed his lips gently to my forehead. "I'm someone who cares about you."

"You barely know me."

"I don't have to know you to care about you."

My heart was aflutter. I could no longer feel my knees against the sandy grass. His very touch seemed to lift me into another realm, a soft and mysterious realm where the most wonderful part of living was his touch.

I asked, "What happened...just now?"

"I don't know."

"Steve..."

He didn't give me time to finish. His lips moved softly from my forehead to my cheek and then to my lips, and pressed tenderly against them. I closed my eyes and welcomed the sensations. My heart raced with the excitement of him. My whole being filled with the closeness of him. I knew as sure as I was alive that there was magic in the wonder of him. I didn't understand the magic, but I could feel it course through me. And, I knew, so could he.

The magic had bonded us.

Hand in hand, we explored the river islands for the next hour. In the buoyancy of that enchanted hour, Steve didn't mention any work obligations for the afternoon—nor did we talk about my nightmares or the house.

He asked, "Is there a special someone in your life?"

"Not at the moment."

"But there has been."

"I was married at age twenty-one to my college art professor. I thought he was a great artist. We were separated two years later and divorced three years after that."

"Was he a great artist?"

"He had considerable recognition but at some point it ceased to matter. If he had been a man impersonating a great artist, that would have been all right. But he turned out to be a great artist impersonating a man, and that wasn't all right. We drifted so far apart I never discovered who he really was. Have you ever been married?"

"No. I came close once. She left me."

What woman would leave him? I wondered. "Left you? For another man?"

"No."

He didn't elaborate. I waited, thinking he would, and when the silence became uncomfortable, he muttered, "She had her reasons."

"You sound bitter."

"Yeah, I know. Bitterness is one of my quirks."

"I hope it doesn't carry over to all women."

"I've been told often enough that it does."

At least he was honest. He'd been badly burned for reasons he wouldn't discuss. Deliberately or not, he was telling me why he was still single.

And bitter or not, a certain gentleness in this man had surfaced this afternoon. More than gentleness—a tenderness. I felt privileged to have seen this side of Steve Hayes; my instinct told me few people ever had. On the exterior he was friendly enough, but he was tough. Maybe he loved his wide wild river sanctuary because here he could shed his shell and tune into nature and his real self. Whatever had happened in his life had caused a thick outer shell to form.

The subject of our failed pasts was lost to pleasures of the moment. We made our way through slabs of sunlight that shone through the leaves hugging the tall willow limbs. The river island narrowed where the river ran deeper and more swiftly. "These are deer tracks!" I said when we paused on a shelf of sun-dried sand. "And over there, raccoon!" I ran ahead of him. "And here—a turtle crawled across right here."

"You're pretty good."

"I'm right? I am? I don't know how I knew!"

"You're a puzzle to me, Karen. You're a woman full of mystery."

"So are you, Mayor Hayes. Do you know how many people in your fair little city get edgy at the mere mention of your name? Oh, no, don't look at me like that; it's not my imagination. People get edgy and shifty when I bring up your name and they tell me you hate publicity. A mayor who hates publicity. I find a certain mystery in that."

I expected him to express surprise at my revelation. He didn't; he merely smiled. "We have no need for publicity in this valley. I can't play at politics because there aren't any challengers to play with." He plunged his hands into his pockets. "I didn't go after this job—it was laid on me. But since I've got it, I do it my way."

"People like you, but they act a little scared of you."

"I think you're imagining that," he said.

"Then what is it if it isn't fear? I bring up your name and people get nervous."

"They think you're a reporter."

"So? What difference would that make? You're a man in public life."

Steve himself was becoming evasive now; I could feel it. "Then that's the reason," he said.

I shook my head. Steve knew why people reacted as they did, but he wasn't about to tell me, not now, probably not ever. I wouldn't be here long enough to ever really know him. But if I were to make a judgment on what

I'd seen, Steve had some kind of control here, some kind of hold on these people, and they didn't like an outsider getting too close.

As we walked, he abruptly shifted the subject away from himself. "My cousin Glen grew up in Tyrone and I didn't. He's spent more of his adult life here than I have, so he knows this town better. He might remember something about the Saxons or know who would. Do you object to talking to him?"

"Of course not."

"Glen is six years older than I. He was already out of high school when I moved back here after my mother died, so we didn't spend much time together. I was only twelve then."

"Would a whole generation put up a wall of silence to hide something?"

"Hell yes. In this town."

"Even from you?"

"Maybe especially from me."

"But why?"

"If I knew that..." He shrugged.

Steve paused. He leaned against the trunk of a cottonwood tree and pulled me close. "You confuse me, lady," he said, stroking my cheek lightly with the backs of his fingers. "You show up here out of the blue, out of nowhere, and I feel like I've known you all my life."

"Since we've been here at the river, I've felt that, too—felt I've known you. I feel like I've walked these little islands long, long ago, and the river knows who I am."

The dreamy look in his eyes matched the expression I'd seen in those moments when he was holding water for me to drink. I heard the gurgle of his river and the warbling of birds and I felt the sun on our shoulders when he kissed me and held me in his arms.

STEVE DROPPED ME AT my car before he returned to his office in midafternoon. I recall the fragrance of honeysuckle carried on a soft breeze as I sat in my car with the windows rolled down, trying to define the barrier between illusion and reality. Steve's kiss had left me stunned. My own reaction to his kiss stunned me even more. I had wanted to cling to him as if I were clinging to safety and to sanity while my heart was thundering into a place far beyond safety. The mere presence of another person had never meant so much to me. I wanted to be with him. Heaven help me, I wanted him. I'd never been so wildly attracted to a man in my life. And knowing the attraction was mutual made it even worse.

I started the engine finally and began to drive aimlessly up and down streets, acquainting myself with this pretty little town that nestled snugly in the valley of the wide and rambling Pawnee River.

At the entrance to a cemetery on the edge of town, I pulled up and stopped. A wild notion struck me. If Mary Saxon had died as Cecilia said, she might have been buried in Tyrone. What better agenda offered itself for the rest of the afternoon than a stroll through the town's graveyard?

The sun was hot on my shoulders as I walked over the velvet green grass reading Tyrone family names on marble stones. Some names appeared over and over again. MacDonald, Pickett, Hayes. The tombstones of Steve's relatives were clustered near two enormous chestnut trees.

I had almost given up the idea of finding any proof of Mary Saxon's death by the time I came upon two small tombstones marked Saxon in a remote part of the cemetery. Something pulled in my chest. So pathetic, they were, so insignificant and devoid of design, save for the names—Mary Louise Saxon, Wayne Randolf Saxon. No birthdates, only the dates of death. The dates were the same! Twenty-five years ago.

I sat down on a nearby bench and tried to make sense of this. The Saxons had died the same day? And here was that five-year gap again! The couple had not left Tyrone as several people had implied. They had died on the same day—about the time Daphne Hayes bought their house! This didn't add up.

What had happened? An accident? Murder? A double murder? Could the husband have murdered the wife, as the old rumor went, and then he was killed by someone else that same day? Lynched without a trial, maybe? Could that be it?

No, I thought, there was no evidence that a murder ever took place. *So why do I know one did? My dream has told me it did and I believe my dream.*

"Dear God," I muttered aloud as I sat on the bench in the hush of the still graveyard, looking across the lawn at the two silent tombs. *I believe my dream!* Leafy shadows fingered across the cold marble stones, blocking the warmth of summer sun. If only those stones could talk!

Twenty-five years ago a double funeral had taken place here in the Tyrone cemetery, and no one claimed to remember it. Surely a funeral home or one of the churches would have some record of it? I rose from the bench and hurried back to my car.

Pulling away from the curb, I noticed a floral shop in the small cluster of stores across the street. Impulsively I swung around and pulled in.

Ten minutes later I found myself back at the cemetery, placing a bouquet of sweet fresh flowers on each of those two lonely graves. I didn't know what compelled me to do such a thing, but the compulsion was undeniable. Who were they? I asked myself over and over. Who were the people who lay under these long-abandoned stones? Whose lives, and whose deaths, lay unacknowledged by a whole town?

Why did the loneliness of these graves cause an ache in my heart so deep I lingered for long minutes watching the breeze tickle the petals of my pitiful offering of flowers? They had been alive, like me. They had spent summer nights on the porch of their beautiful home, and winter evenings by the fire. They'd had dreams, like all of us. Until some horrible, unspeakable thing had happened to them. My eyes filled with tears that blurred the colors of the flowers on the dismal graves.

I HAD BARELY RETURNED to my hotel room when Steve phoned.

"Are you ready to go for a drive with Glen and me?"

"I think I can probably fit it into my social agenda," I answered. "Where are we going?"

"I'll explain when we get there. Twenty minutes, okay?"

Twenty minutes gave me time to shower and change from my summer slacks into a lavender cotton dress and sandals. I was waiting in front of the motel when Steve drove up, not in his pickup, but in a late-model automobile. His cousin Glen was in the back seat drinking beer.

We were headed for a ranch in the south hills, they told me, to talk to a man named McGil, and on the way back we were going to stop at a steak house for dinner.

Glen Hadsell was in high spirits. "This guy McGil," he explained, "he knew Wayne Saxon. One day when I was about twelve I was in town with my dad for a livestock sale. Afterward this guy from Lovitt, up north, was telling my dad about some kind of altercation between Saxon and McGil over the sale of a horse. As I recall it,

Saxon accused McGil of lying to him about the condition of a horse he sold him, and somebody who looked at the horse took Saxon's side. I don't remember what happened, but I remember the fight."

Steve said, "McGil doesn't socialize with anybody in Tyrone, never has, so we figured he might be one person who wouldn't suffer the epidemic memory loss—although, living out of town, he might not know any more than anybody else about why the Saxons left Tyrone."

"The Saxons didn't leave," I said. "Wayne and Mary Saxon died here, on the same day, twenty-five years ago."

Glen sat forward. Steve looked over at me. "How the devil did you learn that?"

"I decided to look in the cemetery this afternoon and I found their tombstones."

"Wow!" Glen breathed. "Tombstones? With the same date?"

I nodded. "Mary and Wayne."

Glen said, "If they died on the same day, that means something happened—"

"Yeah," Steve cut in. "And how the hell could everybody forget what it was?"

Glen was breathing down my neck. "They couldn't! Something is mighty strange here."

"Obviously a cover-up to protect somebody."

"Somebody of the old guard!" Glen said. "And they're solidly united in the effort. Old Tyrone unites well, always could, right, cuz?"

I sensed a second meaning in Glen's words, a reference directed at Steve. Whatever the hidden meaning, Steve ignored it.

"I find it interesting," I said, "that although you're not part of that old guard, as you call it, neither of you ever saw those tombstones."

Steve was the first to reply. "I've never had cause to go through the cemetery, except for an occasional funeral."

"Me, neither," Glen piped in.

"So you see, any suspicions there are groundless," Steve concluded.

Still, I couldn't quiet another thought—no matter how rude—that kept coming to mind. "How could you have run unopposed for mayor?"

"The old guard is of another generation, getting too old to run things now, and very few of them are left. Who told you I ran unopposed, by the way?"

"The librarian—Kimberly Johnstone."

Glen made a little whistling sound. "Whoa. Kimberly! Erv Eckles's girlfriend...though why she'd go for Eckles, I'll never know."

"I met Ervin Eckles at the sheriff's office," I said. "He seems like a nice guy to me."

"Cuz Glen is speaking from the curse of jealously," Steve explained. "He's had his own designs on Kimberly."

Glen didn't deny this, in spite of the fact that he was almost old enough to be her father. It was hard to decide whether these two men liked one another or merely tolerated one another; they sent off very mixed signals.

The ride over a narrow gravel hill road took forty minutes while the day deepened into twilight. We discussed the Saxons for most of the ride and the house they had abandoned. Glen had never been inside the house. According to him, few people had.

Steve swung off the gravel road onto a small side road that looked like little more than a cattle trail. It continued for half a mile before a gate appeared with a weathered overhead sign that said Broken M Ranch with the brand burned into the wood.

Tate McGil was expecting us. He rose from his chair on the front porch of the two-story frame ranch house. As we drove up, a woman appeared at the screen door. We heard shouts of children playing in the meadow beyond, grandchildren probably, who lived in the second house on the ranch, only a few hundred yards from the first. The McGils were elderly and simply dressed. They welcomed us into their sitting room where we were offered lemon- ade.

During the drive up, we had decided on our approach. Steve began as soon as he had introduced me. "Karen is interested in learning more about some of the history of Tyrone," he said. "She's particularly interested in the old Saxon house and the people who lived there."

Tate McGil lit a pipe, slowly, patiently. "Has that place ever sold?"

"No. My grandmother still owns it."

McGil looked at me. "What's your interest in the Saxons?"

"My interest is mainly in the house. I've been trying to determine how long that family lived in it and why they left."

McGil looked at his wife, then curiously at Glen. "Why come all the way out here to talk to us? Why not ask the people in Tyrone? Why not ask Glen here?"

I wondered if Steve noticed the strange knowing look McGil cast at Glen. *These two know each other better than Glen's led us to believe. What kind of game is Glen Hadsell playing? Is Steve in on the game, too?*

"How the hell would I know anything about it?" Glen protested. "I was just a kid."

"No one remembers," I told McGil.

He smirked. "They don't remember, eh? Well now. What makes you think I would?"

Glen was sipping the lemonade in gentlemanly fashion, a role I hadn't seen him play until now. He had been in previous contact with McGil, I was sure of it.

He spoke up, "I recall one time when I was a kid hearing some men discuss an argument between you and Wayne Saxon over a horse. I couldn't tell you the details of that story, but I did recall that you at least knew the man, which is more than anybody else will admit to."

"You recollect good, Glen. Yep, we got into it, all right, over a little buckskin mare I sold him. Wayne Saxon was no horseman. I thought he was looking for a good piece of horseflesh, but he was scared silly of that little mare. Turned out he wanted some gentle nag for his kid to ride."

I sat forward. "The Saxons had a child? A girl or a boy?"

"I seen a kid with him once. Wiry little kid in a big cowboy hat, little bit of a tyke he was."

Mrs. McGil set a plate of cookies on the table in front of us. "That must've been near thirty years ago." She looked at him, offering me a cookie. "Them people died. It's all Tyrone was whispering about for months."

Chapter Seven

Mrs. McGil's words reverberated like an echo around the room. *It's all Tyrone was whispering about for months.* And now, one generation later, forgotten?

"How did they die?" Glen asked.

There was no hesitation on the part of the McGils to discuss a subject no one down in Tyrone would touch. They were, after all, not part of that town. Tate McGil answered, "Wayne Saxon shot his wife and then himself. Nobody ever knew why. If I recall, there was no note or nothing." He glanced at his wife. "Isn't that right, Marj? No note, no explanation—"

"Then the rumors are true!" I exclaimed. Cecilia's story was true and Maude O'Grady knew it and had lied.

"I don't get it," Steve said. "If such a bizarre crime took place, why don't people talk about it? Why would they pretend it never happened?"

"You got me there, Steve. I always said it was a strange bunch down there in that town of yours."

Images of my dream rushed to me. *The hands.*

Feeling Steve's eyes on me, knowing he, too, was thinking of what I had described to him, I asked, "What happened to the Saxon's little child?"

"Never heard no more about him. Did you, Marj?"

"No," Mrs. McGil answered, frowning. "I never heard a word." She played nervously with her gold wedding band, the only jewelry she wore. "I ain't thought about that tragedy in years. Awful, it was. We live out here in the hills and do our trading in Lovitt and don't get to Tyrone much, but I remember that summer. I remember talking to some ladies in the feed store and them saying nobody knew exactly what happened."

"Saxon wasn't the type, I'll say that," her husband confirmed. "Mind, I barely knew the man. Just had that one sorry business transaction with him, but he didn't seem like a violent man, nor anything close to it."

"Nice-looking man," Mrs. McGil offered. "Nice manners, too. Never seen his wife, but they said she was pretty and a whole lot younger than him."

"You wouldn't happen to know the name of his son?" I asked.

"No," McGil answered, puffing slowly on his pipe. "I never saw the tyke but that once. He was sitting in the car, waiting in front of the bank while his pa and me talked."

I didn't like the look in Steve's eyes as he studied the old rancher through a cloud of pipe smoke. It frightened me. I knew Steve's interest had gone beyond me and my dream. He was determined to learn what a whole town— his town—was hiding, and why.

I strongly suspected by now that whatever Steve Hayes went after he ultimately got. And he was going after the truth behind one of the most guarded secrets of Tyrone. Steve's eyes told me that, before I left this town, I would know the secret of the Saxon house; but this knowledge didn't make me feel better. It filled me with a terrible dread.

THE COYOTE'S TRAIL was a roadside steak house, located several miles north of Tyrone. It was rustic, dimly lit, noisy with the background of country music, and it attracted its customers from a wide radius because of its famous Nebraska T-bone steaks. Glen was animated after we left the McGil ranch; Steve was almost sullen. He said very little until we were sitting with steaks the size of dinner plates in front of us.

Glen waved his fork in the air. "The McGils could be lying."

"Why would they lie?"

"Who knows? But you said yourself there ain't nothing about this crime in any official files. If everybody was talking about it, how come I don't remember that, huh? I was thirteen. I can remember back that far."

Busy cutting his steak, Steve looked up at his cousin. "How well do you know McGil?"

"No better than you."

"That wasn't my feeling tonight."

"I can't stand the man, and it's mutual. Him and my dad had some adjoining land and they argued a lot because McGil overgrazed the land and didn't keep his fences up."

"What land is that?"

"A narrow strip on the north side of the river. Actually it belonged to Mrs. McGil's family originally. You didn't know about it, huh?"

Steve looked suspicious. "Do they still have that land?"

"Yeah."

"I see. And I suppose you've spoken to McGil about your development project."

"Only in passing."

"Sure," Steve said sarcastically. "Only in passing. I gather he refuses to sell the land."

"Cuzzie, that has nothing to do with this Saxon thing. McGil is a louse. He accused me of theft once when I was a kid."

"Was his accusation justified?"

"What do you think?"

"What'd you steal?"

"Just a little silver trim off a saddle. My dad covered for me, but old McGil, he's always been a troublemaker. I think he was lying tonight about everything."

"Look," Steve said irritably, "it was your idea to go out there. If you weren't going to believe him, why the hell did we bother?"

Glen's lower lip puckered. "Did you believe him?"

"Yeah. I did."

Glen looked at me. "Did you, Karen?"

"Yes. We know the couple died and on the same day. Their deaths weren't natural."

"We've been lied to, right enough," Steve said, "but not by the McGils."

Glen's mouth was full. He swallowed, nearly choked and reached for his beer. "You're taking the word of old Tate McGil over the word of everybody else, including your own kin?"

Steve's teeth ground in anger. "McGil is the only one who's even had anything to say!"

"He doesn't have credibility."

"And Chuck Dyer does? Standing behind that silver badge declaring how he can't remember why the Saxons left or when? It turns out our sheriff isn't honest, and I don't like that. Not one little bit."

Downing his second beer, Glen was getting perturbed and feisty. "Well, hell, cuz, you and me know things aren't always what they seem. Your foxy lawyer's education is an example. And that hotsy title of yours that Karen must be so impressed with. Nope, things aren't always what they seem."

Steve's eyes flashed. "I strongly suggest you back off before you push me too far. When you drink your mouth runs like a muddy river."

Glen looked at me. "Touchy, ain't he? His Honor the Mayor is touchy."

I sat in discomfort and disgust. Between these two men a burning coal sparked under the surface ready to flare up at the least provocation. Glen had started it, and Steve hadn't acted surprised that he had, but Steve was sensitive to my presence. I trusted he wouldn't make things worse if he could help it.

What had Glen's remark about Steve's education meant? The remark had angered Steve more than he wanted to show. I wondered what was really going on between these two men. I even wondered about myself—what the devil was I doing here sitting beside two strangers, one who didn't seem a stranger and made me feel peaceful in a way I couldn't explain, and the other who had the exact opposite effect on me?

Trying to control the impatience that strained his voice, Steve said, "I confided in you because I thought you'd be helpful, which you have been. You didn't mention a personal feud with McGil."

"I ain't got a personal feud with McGil. I just don't trust him, that's all. Don't forget, I've lived in this valley all my life and you've been here hardly any of yours."

"That's precisely why I needed your help."

"Right. Well then, listen to me. McGil is a rattler."

Glen shrugged and waved his empty glass at the waitress across the room. "Maybe they're right about the

Saxons. Maybe they aren't. I'm just cautioning you, that's all."

Steve sighed heavily. "Now that we've got this much information, the rest should be obtainable somehow."

"And look into it we will, with fervor. Fer-*vor.*" Glen turned to me. "Cousin Steve gets whatever he wants around this valley. Have you noticed all the scabbed and scraped chins around town? They're caused from bowing and scraping to His Honor."

Glen was clearly out of line. The matter was no business of mine, but it was hard to keep silent. I asked him, "Did you vote for Steve for mayor?"

"Damn right I did. We all did. He was the man for the job."

"Then why are you so resentful about his holding that office?"

"Me? Resentful? Nah. He does a good job, old cuz does. And he's saving the river. Heaven help anybody who breaks one stick in the Pawnee River or leaves a footprint in the sand."

"You are resentful," I said softly.

Steve had made a don't-come-over-here motion to the waitress, preventing Glen from ordering another beer. Luckily Glen was too involved in his defense to see the gesture.

"The thing all boils down to the matter of secrets," Glen said, leaning far forward on one elbow. "Secrets can be defined in three major classes. There's class one—the kind that does harm to a lot of people, like improper disposal of nuclear waste. Class two—that's the kind that protects one person at the expense of another, you know, like setting somebody up to take the blame for something he didn't do. And then there's class three—when you keep information from a party who has a right to know. And class four, that's when you keep a secret because you're ashamed to talk about it for fear of what people will think."

"That's four classes," Steve said sourly.

"Yeah, four. I meant four classes." He paused to take another mouthful of beer, then slammed down his mug. "So which class does this Saxon conspiracy come under? That's what we've got to find out. My thinking is it's a class four."

"I don't think so," Steve said. "Unless the person they're protecting is Wayne Saxon. And that wouldn't make sense. Why would anyone lie to protect a dead man?"

"Maybe he's alive."

"You're drunk, Glen."

"So? What's that got to do with Wayne Saxon being alive? Maybe he's somewhere in disguise. Maybe he's still in Tyrone, disguised as one of them Gypsies you chased out of the river."

Steve looked at me and smiled. "I've never chased Gypsies out of the river."

"If you had, you'd have recognized Saxon," Glen said.

Steve threw his napkin onto the table. "Karen, are you ready to go? Let's go."

"Class-four secret," Glen said. "That's *your* class, cuz. Wayne Saxon is class three and you're class four. He's one above you."

"If I ever buy you another beer," Steve said, "Satan has my permission to claim us both." He went directly to the cashier, asked for the check and paid it without looking back at his cousin, who was fumbling around in his pockets.

I could see that Steve was embarrassed, less by the way Glen was acting than by what he had said—making an issue of the fact that Steve had secrets of his own. I guessed that Glen's motive was jealousy, but it was only a guess. It could have been some kind of revenge for all I knew. Either way, I doubted Glen was as drunk as he pretended. I'd guessed a long time ago that Steve was concealing something about himself.

WITH THE STEREO playing softly from the rear speakers, Glen nodded off in the back seat. About five miles from Tyrone, Steve turned onto a road that detoured west toward the Hadsell ranch.

It was too dark to see much. Lights were in the windows of the two-story house. All the outer buildings were nestled in silence. When the car stopped, Glen stirred and yawned. He sat up and looked around.

"What'd you bring me home for, cuz? My truck's at your place."

"I'll send somebody out with it in the morning. You're in no shape to drive tonight."

Another yawn. "For once you're right, cuz. I salute you. Keep up the pursuit of truth and justice." He opened the car door. "G'night, Karen."

"Say hello to Amy," Steve said.

"Hello to Amy," Glen repeated loudly.

When we were back on the dark road heading for town, I asked, "Who is Amy?"

"Glen's wife."

"I didn't realize he was married."

"Amy's his second wife. She stays home all the time. I rarely see her."

"His remarks about Kimberly...?"

"Were out of line. Glen spends half his time out of line. He never let marriage interfere with his flirtations. That's why his first wife divorced him."

Glen's accusing remarks about Steve had given root to a lot of questions I wanted to ask. Steve had spent so little of his life in Tyrone, Glen had said. Steve's widowed mother had moved away when he was young and he returned at age twelve to live with his grandmother; this much I knew. Intuition warned me to be careful about questions, lest I tread on ground too close to Steve's secret—class-four secret—whatever that meant. Steve had a right to privacy and it was beneath me to use Glen's ravings as a motivation for probing into Steve's personal life. Still, he wouldn't resent a polite interest after what we had shared at the river.

Darkness surrounded us as we drove, save for the cones of our headlights on the narrow road. The darkness was heavy, thick; it seemed the car had to plow through it. There was no other traffic on the road.

"You said you left Tyrone as a child."

"I went to high school here."

"And then left for college."

"Yeah."

"Why did you return after you graduated from law school? Why did you choose to live in Tyrone?"

"It's as good a place as any."

I couldn't read his face in the darkness, but the subject of his own past put a strain in his voice. I sensed his answer to my last question was not an answer at all. There had been some other reason he'd come back to this town. Some other reason he had run for mayor. Glen had hinted at it, and I could sense it. But I didn't dare ask. There would be no point, because he wouldn't tell me.

Steve's secrets would remain hidden behind his charming smile and his mysterious eyes.

At one-thirty in the morning Steve pulled into the driveway of the motel under the dim blinking glow of its red neon sign, and parked in front of my room.

"At least we have a place to start now," he said.

"I couldn't get anywhere without you."

"You found the tombstones without me." He touched my hair, then my cheek. I couldn't hear his breathing, but I could feel it as he moved away from the steering wheel and close to me, his breathing in sync with mine. In the darkness, his presence was so powerful my mind reeled.

Softly his lips devoured mine. His kiss, light at first, deepened into intimacy far beyond the limitations of a kiss. I clung to him. In response his arms tightened around me. His arms, his kiss, felt so good. So right.

"Karen..." he whispered. "Ever since I first saw you, I haven't been able to stop thinking about you. What is it about you that intrigues me so?"

"What is it about you..." I whispered back. "You put me at ease when everything else around me is so crazy."

"You make me feel at ease, too. You and I are real, but none of the rest of this is."

"Glen was way out of line tonight, and it angered you, but you didn't start trouble over it."

"I didn't because of you."

"I know." Then I asked, "Are people afraid of you?"

"I don't know why they would be. I have a temper but I control it."

"Always?"

"Almost always." He held me closer. "I don't want to talk about me. It's late and we've both got projects for tomorrow. It isn't fair to keep you up any later. I'll just reluctantly say good-night...."

When we kissed again, our spirits soared together to a realm beyond the reality of Tyrone. If we had prolonged the kiss, I'd have easily forgotten everything in the world but him... but us.

As if on some invisible signal, we both drew away. I fumbled for the door handle. My knees were trembling when I stepped out into the cool of the deep night.

I was half-undressed in my room, three or four minutes later, before I heard the sputter of his engine starting.

My mind was so on overload I couldn't fall asleep. Too much was happening too fast.

There had always been—at least in my conscious memory—an unidentifiable emptiness inside of me that no one had ever been able to touch—not my parents, nor my husband when I'd loved him, nor anyone. I'd called that emptiness by several names, trying to define it. I'd called it *longing* and I'd called it *loneliness*. I've never been a lonely person, really, but once in a while, at unexpected times, that emptiness would gnaw through and I'd experience a terrible longing for something just out of reach.

Tonight, by some miracle, Steve's kiss had pierced that quiet still place far down inside me. And I was shaken. It was more than my sexual attraction to him, which, God knew, was strong. This was a deeper thing, and unexplainable.

WE HAD MADE A PLAN for the next day. I was going to contact the funeral home and each of the town's four churches to see if any records existed concerning the funeral. It might even be possible to shake some memories free if I persisted. A funeral for the Saxons must have taken place, and someone must have been in charge of the arrangements.

Steve planned to do his detective work at the sheriff's office and the courthouse. As mayor, he'd have easier access to records. Death certificates, an accounting of the suicide and especially of the murder, had to exist somewhere, if the McGils' story was true. People's bodies can be buried more easily than the legal evidence of their lives can be buried.

The office of the funeral home was unoccupied. I had to call into the back hallway to rouse someone. To my disappointment the gentleman in dark clothes who finally materialized was in his forties, not old enough to have handled the Saxon funeral. He was unaccustomed to anyone walking in unannounced, so I quickly introduced myself and told him what I wanted.

"None of our records go back twenty-five years," Shelby Williams told me. "The business changed hands sixteen years ago, after the former owner, Alfred Coffee, died, and I have no information on any transactions before that time."

"What happened to the earlier records, Mr. Williams?"

"They were destroyed. Obsolete. Exactly what is it you're looking for?"

"Hopefully the name of a family member who was in charge of arrangements. Names of anyone involved who would know more about these people."

The funeral home director unbuttoned and buttoned the waist of his jacket repeatedly, a nervous gesture that was beginning to distract me. "I wish I could be of help," he said.

"Yes, so do I. If you should come across any information, would you mind getting in touch with Steve Hayes at the mayor's office?"

He blinked in surprise. "What interest does Mayor Hayes have in this?"

"Nothing personal. He's just helping me."

Bitterly disappointed, I thanked Shelby Williams and left. With notebook in hand, in which I'd written the names and addresses of the town's churches, I went around to each. Not one of the personnel found anything helpful in church records. I hit a dead end. No evidence seemed to exist anywhere. It would have been easy to discount that murder/suicide story if I hadn't seen the tombstones.

My futile investigation took a good part of the day. In midafternoon I found myself once again at the library.

Kimberly Johnstone greeted me with enthusiasm. "Karen! I heard you're still looking for information about the people who lived in the Sycamore Street house."

"Where did you hear that?"

"Glen Hadsell told me. And I also heard it from my boyfriend."

"Things get around Tyrone fast."

"Like a brushfire."

"Is your boyfriend Ervin Eckles, the deputy sheriff?"

"How did you know?"

I smiled. "Flames of the brushfire. I met Ervin yesterday at the sheriff's office when I was inquiring about crime files."

Kimberly was wearing a crisp summer dress of pink cotton, cut low in front and fitted in the bodice. She sat on one of the library tables, dangling her sandaled feet. "Is it true there was a murder in the Saxon house?"

"We've been able to find no evidence that it's true," I answered, sitting at the opposite end of the table, fatigued and discouraged after a day of dead ends. "No police records, no funeral records and no memories jarred loose by our questions."

Kimberly lowered her voice, even though we were alone in the book-lined room. "When I was a little kid, I heard about a murder in that house. There's always been a rumor surrounding it. I always thought it was just part of the ghost story."

"Maybe it is, for all we know." I thought, the McGils might have heard those rumors and remembered them as fact. Yet they had said the town talked about it for months. Either they were lying or everybody else was.

"I heard you found their graves."

"Yes." I wondered just how many people Glen had been talking to this morning. Whispers of my quest were all over town. That sure wasn't going to help.

"Erv said he talked to Steve Hayes this morning," she said. "Erv is going to do everything he can to find out something. If there is anything to find out, Erv can do it."

"His help is greatly appreciated." I drew a deep breath. "Kimberly, I stopped in here to get off my feet in a cool place. Tromping around in the heat is wearing me out. I also wanted to ask if there is anything in the library on women's groups or anything Mary Saxon might have participated in. It's a desperate long shot, but worth a try. I might learn who her friends were. Some of them must still live here. Someone who cared about her, if not about her husband."

"I can't think of anything, but I'll give some thought to it. I can tell you this—Erv said Chuck Dyer was a deputy sheriff back then and he'd *have* to remember!"

"Steve thinks so, too. There's something else. The Saxons had a son."

"Who told you that?"

"A rancher north of town. Tate McGil."

"Oh, yes! Glen mentioned McGil. He said it wasn't much to go on—the McGils' story, I mean."

"I think the story is true. And I wonder what became of that child. That's the other information I'm digging for, Kimberly—where is that child now?"

"Nobody named Saxon has lived in this town as long as I can remember."

"Relatives must have taken him. I have to assume no one around here adopted him."

"Maybe someone did," she said, "and everybody's trying to protect him so he won't have to know that his father killed his mother."

I looked at her with new respect. "That's a reasonable assumption. It could very well be."

"I don't know who he'd be, though."

I felt a little shiver go up my spine as I remembered that everyone had lied to Steve about the Saxon matter. Surely not... No, it couldn't be! Steve was about the same age as the Saxon's son, but he was Daphne Hayes's grandson. And Daphne Hayes was not a Saxon.

Steve's father had died when Steve was a very young boy and his mother when he was twelve.

Had I missed a third Saxon grave? A telltale sign of a wider tragedy than any of us had imagined? I filed away the thought for later.

When I got back to the motel around four o'clock, the owner, Wanda Clark, came to my room with a message. She handed me a white envelope with only my name written on the front in a large bold handwriting.

"It was brought by a messenger," Wanda said.

Certain the note was from Steve asking me to phone him when I got in, I tore open the envelope.

The note was neatly typed on white paper, but it was not from Steve. A new and unfamiliar fear gripped my heart. I felt the blood drain from my face.

Chapter Eight

It has come to our intention that you are diligently pursuing information about Tyrone and its citizens. Whether this information is to be published or not, we wish to inform you that such inquiries are not welcome. We are a private town, like a family, and we will not tolerate intrusion by anyone from outside into our private business.

If such activity on your part continues, we will be forced to take action against you. We suggest you leave at once, before this action is necessary. Do not force our hand on this very serious matter.

Citizens Auxiliary Committee

When I looked up from reading the letter, Wanda Clark was staring at me. "What is it?" she asked. "Is something wrong?"

"It's from the Citizens Auxiliary Committee."

"What's that?"

"You haven't heard of it?"

She shook her head. "Must be one of those snooty women's groups from over on the east side of town. They've always got some cause or another over there. What do they want?"

"They want me to leave town immediately, or else."

Her eyes widened. Her hand came over her heart. "Or else what?"

"That isn't clear. They're hinting about some kind of legal action."

"For what?"

"For asking too many questions about the family who used to live in the empty house on Sycamore Street." That wasn't precisely what the letter said, but I knew that was its intent.

Wanda's brow wrinkled. "I don't understand!"

"I don't understand, either. The Saxon family hasn't lived in Tyrone for a quarter of a century. I can't imagine why people who don't even claim to remember them care so much about my questions now."

The telephone on the table beside the bed jangled. I picked it up, glancing at Mrs. Clark.

Steve's voice was like a rush of warmth after the spurt of fright caused by the letter. "When are you free for dinner?" he asked. "How soon can I pick you up?"

I looked at my watch. "Give me thirty or forty minutes to shower and change."

"I thought we'd have dinner at my house if that's okay with you."

"I'd like that." More than he knew, I thought. After this letter, I wasn't anxious to be seen in public, especially with the mayor, and especially not before Steve was aware of the fact that someone was trying to run me out of town.

"Great. I'll give you forty minutes. We'll talk then."

Mrs. Clark looked at me strangely. "Sounds as if you have a dinner invitation."

"Yes." I smiled. "I've found the people in Tyrone to be very friendly. With, of course, the glaring excepting of—" I waved the letter "—the Citizens Auxiliary."

"Citizens Auxiliary," she repeated sourly. "It sounds like a bunch of busybodies to me. Hooty-tooties with nothing better to do. Somebody around here has a weird itch, but I can't think who." She stepped toward the open door. "For my part, you're welcome to stay here as long as you like."

"Thanks," I said. "I plan to be here several more days at least."

Steve's house, like just about everything else in Tyrone, was only a five-minute drive from the motel. On the way he discussed, of all things, the weather. A storm front, he said, was moving down from the Dakotas and was expected to hit before morning.

"The wind will probably be coming up soon," he said as he pulled into his driveway, "so we won't delay our barbecue too long. The storm would ruin my plans. These seasonal summer storms on the prairie can be wicked."

Skipper met us in the driveway. His tail thumped my leg as he greeted us with yips and wiggling. When we started for the front door, the dog ran along the side of the house, squirmed under a gate into the back yard and disappeared.

From a narrow foyer we entered a living room furnished with a few pieces of period furniture. Two large paintings and a mirror with an antique frame adorned the walls. Except for one exquisite table lamp, there was nothing on the tables, not a single knickknack or book. Nothing personal was in this room.

"It's lovely," I said. "These beautiful antiques sit so well in here."

"They sit well because they've been here forever. The house was furnished with these period pieces after it was built in 1932, and the owners lived here until they died and never changed a thing. I bought it the way they left it."

"I don't blame you for not changing anything."

Leading me through the dining room and into the kitchen, which had a charming breakfast nook in one corner, he said, "I did add modern appliances. When you're a bachelor, a microwave is a necessity."

"Do you like the bachelor's life?"

"I profoundly prefer it to the alternative."

"You've never tried the alternative."

"And I'm not inclined to."

I didn't say so, but I felt he'd been badly burned. "Inclinations are funny things. They can cool like coals."

He smiled. "Which reminds me we have a barbecue to attend to. Come this way."

The back door, leading to a large fenced yard, was open. People in Tyrone evidently didn't bother much with locks. Opening the door, he motioned me outside. The squeaking of the screen door sent a rush of nostalgia through me. Summer evenings of home. The feel of the air before a summer storm. I knew I could learn to love it here.

"I'll get the coals started," Steve said, and as he busied himself with the preparations, Skipper tore around the yard happily, trying to get his master's attention.

When he had started the coals and thrown the ball a few times for the dog to catch, we went back inside, where he mixed us a drink. This time, Skipper followed.

"He's allowed in the back of the house, but not in the front," Steve explained. "I try to keep dog hairs off the living room furniture for the benefit of people in dark clothes who might want to sit in there.''

A few steps up from the kitchen was a den, which was built over the garage. It had a plate-glass window overlooking the back yard. Steve didn't have to tell me that this room was where he spent his time. Bookcases covered an entire wall. There was a television and stereo here, magazines scattered about, and a collection of football and boxing trophies bunched together on a shelf. The furniture was dark-stained oak in Cape Cod style, sturdy and masculine. A rug in front of the sofa was fuzzed white with a layer of dog hair.

"This is more comfortable than sitting in the back yard with the wind blowing smoke in our faces.'' Steve motioned me to the couch and sat down beside me. "Now. You first. Tell me what you found out today.''

"I found out that the funeral home has no records, the churches have nothing in their files about a funeral or marriage or baptism or anything to do with the Saxons. There's nothing in school records on the child—he evidently was too young to be in school. But I do wonder if the boy died. His tombstone wasn't in the cemetery, I know that. I found only the tombstones of his parents. But then, again, he might be buried somewhere else.''

Steve nodded, and threw up his hands. "Then we're where we started. We'd still have to locate him. Whether alive or dead.''

After a moment, I resumed. "Did you have better luck today?''

He glanced up, the warmth in his eyes sending a warm chill through me. "I rechecked police files. Sheriff Dyer made a fake play of wanting to be helpful, but if I read Chuck correctly, he's squirming about our questions around town. His deputy, Erv, *is* interested. He's digging into every crack he can think of. I asked him to investigate as quietly as possible.''

"It's too late to be discreet. The whole town's alerted, and some of the people don't like it."

"Only the ones who are covering up something, whatever it is."

"The Citizens Auxiliary Committee."

"Huh? What are you talking about?" He looked angry, startled.

I took the envelope from my handbag and handed it to him.

He frowned. "What is this?"

"A letter that was left for me at the motel."

I watched Steve's face carefully as he read. His lips drew tightly together. When he looked up at me, his eyes flared with anger that frightened me.

"There is no such organization!" Steve rose and slammed around the room. The dog, sensing trouble, slid under the table and looked out over his paws, watching every move his master made.

Steve kicked the bottom of an overstuffed chair. "Who the hell do they think they are? Harassing you!"

"This could have been sent by only one person."

"Maybe. I intend to find out who. Whether it's one or a hundred, I won't stand for this!"

"Steve, I think whoever wrote this made a bad move, because it proves beyond any shadow of a doubt a coverup's going on. Before, we were only guessing."

"You're right. It was a very dumb move. Especially if they thought you might show it to me." He swore viciously and then apologized. "I can't even trust the sheriff in this town. I might be forced to take the law into my own hands to get this mess resolved."

"Who could they be trying to protect, Steve? It has to be someone connected with the Saxons. Kimberly and I were discussing this in the library. Glen told her about McGil's story. We came up with a theory if the child's still alive, it's him they are protecting."

"The boy? There's no Saxon left around here."

"Exactly. He might have been adopted by someone in or around Tyrone and they changed his name. Or as I said, he's . . . in the cemetery somewhere."

Steve rubbed his chin as he sat down again. "Umm. That makes a certain amount of sense. I know everybody in this valley, and I can't think of anybody who adopted a kid. . . ."

"You wouldn't remember. You were just a baby yourself then."

"You've got a good theory, Karen, but knowing the people in this valley, I just don't think it's the right one."

"Then who could they be protecting? You don't think Glen could be right about Wayne Saxon being alive, do you? And his tombstone a fake?"

"Why would the town protect a murderer?"

"Maybe they feel the murder was justified." I sighed. "We're grasping at straws."

Picking up the letter from the table where he'd tossed it, Steve studied it carefully. "I wonder if my grandmother has anything to do with this. I never knew anything to go on in this town that she didn't know about, and she's never been willing to tell me the truth about that damned house. Hang on a minute, Karen. I'll be right back. I just want to check those coals."

Through the window I watched him down on the lawn poking at the fire. He looked like a magazine ad in his tight jeans and boots and shirt sleeves rolled up to the elbow—his working clothes. What an unlikely man to be mayor. The people of Tyrone were hesitant to talk about their mayor, as if there was something about him they didn't want me to know. Why *had* they elected him mayor? There was something about his holding the town's highest office that neither he nor anyone else wanted me to know.

He was suddenly at the top of the stairs, reentering the den. "It's been forty-five minutes. The coals look fine. Are you ready?"

I nodded eagerly. "I skipped lunch."

"Good. The sky is getting threatening. The high wind is busy. I think the storm might hit sooner than predicted. How do you like your steak?"

"Medium rare."

"Me, too. This'll be easy, then."

In the kitchen he set out two T-bone steaks, rubbed them with garlic and washed two huge potatoes.

"This reminds me of home," I said. "Steak and baked potatoes."

"And salad, of course."

"I'll make the salad."

"Great. Everything's in the refrigerator. I went shopping on my lunch hour and stormed through the vegetable section. Throw in whatever suits you."

The potatoes went into the microwave. That part was not like the old days.

While Steve tended the steaks in the back yard, I made the salad, found plates and silverware, and set two places at the table in the breakfast nook. Outside the wide French windows of the nook, trees were bending and swooshing in the wind and scraping against the glass. Skipper didn't like the signs of the storm; he came into the kitchen and followed me around.

Thunder rolled lowly and lightning began to flicker in the distance by the time we were finishing our meal. "It's going to be a bad one," Steve said.

"Fits my mood."

"You don't like this town much, do you?"

"I do like Tyrone," I answered. "I mean, it's a lovely little place and I like small towns, but it frightens me."

"The town frightens you? You mean those idiots who wrote you that stupid letter?"

"No. I mean, the town frightens me the same way the house does, only to a smaller degree. These streets frighten me. The crickets at night and the birds singing in the morning. The whole place frightens me."

He scowled. "I don't frighten you, too, do I?"

"No. I don't know why you don't, though. Glen does."

"Glen? Good Lord, why?"

"I don't know, Steve. I honestly don't know. I've been so... on edge ever since I came here. I feel like I'm being followed—there are shadows everywhere. I've never experienced such awful feelings."

He gazed at me thoughtfully. "You weren't frightened at the river yesterday."

"No, not at the river. It was different at the river. And you seemed to know that."

"I was there with you, remember? I kissed you at the river. You were trembling in my arms, but it wasn't from fear."

He reached across the table and took my hand. "There is something about us, Karen. When you walked into my life it was as though you'd always been there. You felt it, too, didn't you?"

"I felt it at the river."

"Do you feel it now?"

"Yes."

His eyes were soft and looked directly into mine. "I don't want you to be afraid. You don't have to be afraid as long as I'm here. Nothing can ever happen to you as long as I'm here."

I believed him. Maybe just because I wanted to. Steve had dark secrets like everybody else in this weird town, and yet I trusted him. Even knowing it wasn't smart to do so, I trusted him. I felt safe with him.

He was still holding my hand when the doorbell rang.

"I hate interruptions," he complained as he rose to answer the door.

I heard voices from the front room, and in a moment Ervin Eckles and Kimberly Johnstone followed Steve into the kitchen.

Unable to hide her surprise at seeing me, Kimberly recovered quickly and broke into a pleased smile. "Sorry to interrupt your dinner."

"We were finished," I said, rising.

Steve said, "Come on up to the den. How about a beer?"

"Never turned down a beer yet," Erv said after greeting me. "Not off duty, anyhow. Where's Skipper? How come the old boy didn't come to the door with you?"

"The storm. As soon as the thunder gets bad, Skip hides under the bed in the guest room, and he wouldn't come out if a family of cats was meowing at the door."

Rain was already slashing the windows of the den. "Those clouds moved in quicker than expected," Ervin said as he lowered himself onto the couch. "Man, we need this rain. It's been a dry summer up to now."

Steve handed them each a beer. "What'll you have, Karen?"

"Nothing. I'm fine."

"Well," Eckles said with a great heave of his chest, "I been a man obsessed since you talked to me this morning, Steve. As a trained lawman, I can smell spoiled fish in the wind, and this whole story of yours ain't smelled good from the start. Something's going on in this town, there ain't no question of it."

"What'd you find?" Steve asked.

"I dug up some old records out of the basement of the county coroner's office. As a deputy, I got access to all those files."

Kimberly reached into her oversize handbag and handed some papers to Steve.

"I took the liberty of lifting them out of the file drawer," Ervin said, "because it's been coming clear to me that somebody's been pulling files and records all over town, and whoever is doing it might remember these. Here's your proof there was a murder."

Steve fell into silence with the limp papers in front of him. Rain slashed the windows, lightning streaked across the sky, and thunder was cracking loudly.

"The Saxon couple died of gunshot wounds," he explained to me, as he read. "Mary Saxon was shot in the heart at close range and Wayne Saxon was shot in the chest and also in the temple with the same gun. The gun was found next to his body."

"Murder and suicide," Ervin said. "Couldn't be much plainer."

Kimberly asked, "How can something like this have happened right here in Tyrone and we've never heard of it?"

"Because somebody has gone to great lengths to cover it up," her boyfriend said.

"They're still at it," Steve said, reaching for the letter on the coffee table. "Take a look at this. It was delivered to Karen this afternoon."

The young deputy's face crinkled as he read. "What? Citizens Auxiliary? What the hell is that?"

"It's the person or persons behind the cover-up."

Kimberly was reading over his shoulder. "Karen, this is shocking! They're trying to scare you into leaving town."

"According to this coroner's report," Steve said, thumbing through the three or four stapled pages, "there was pretty conclusive evidence that Saxon's death was a suicide, which rules out the theory that somebody else killed them both."

"I was thinking along the same lines," Erv said. "But why no police report? What's with Chuck Dyer, Steve? He doesn't remember two bodies dead from bullet wounds? Hah! He ain't that senile!"

I said, "It seems strange that whoever went to all the trouble of cleaning out police files would overlook the coroner's report."

"Not too strange," Eckles corrected. "The coroner at the time requested somebody from the state office in Lincoln to go over his findings, which means there's some record on file in the state office. If anybody ever pulled those files out and our county couldn't produce theirs, it would look real bad. I don't think they dared destroy everything. They just buried these as deep as they could."

Kimberly glowed with pride. "They couldn't bury them too deep for Erv to find."

Steve smiled. "This is good work."

"What can we do with this?" I asked.

Steve sat back, ankle over knee. "We have to start questioning people. There's going to be plenty of squirming, but presented with proof of how the Saxons died, I don't see how they can keep up the amnesia act. What do you think, Erv?"

"I think we might draw up a list of people who could be behind that letter. If that letter is part of the cover-up, then whoever wrote it has to be over fifty and lived in Tyrone when this happened."

"But it just doesn't make sense!" Kimberly said. "*Everybody* who was living here then would remember! How could a whole town cover it up?"

"Maybe everybody didn't know," I offered. "Maybe the cover-up began right then."

"It must have," Steve said. "The McGils talked about rumors and whispers in town, but nobody knew for sure what the story was. They were probably just repeating rumors."

Ervin scratched his head. "We've had a couple run-ins with that old barnacle McGil. He'd lie when the truth would do better. Got a lot of enemies, that one has."

"But he wasn't lying about the murder/suicide."

"Nope. We know now he wasn't lying about that."

"Well," Kimberly said, "even if you get people to admit the Saxons are dead, that doesn't mean they're going to tell you anything else. How will you pry things out of them that they went to such lengths to conceal?"

"Somebody will have to crack," Steve said.

"That might not happen," Ervin insisted, "because there's no simple explanation for this cover-up. And still going on after twenty-five years? Hell, I think these people are all protecting themselves."

Kimberly shifted in her chair like a child who couldn't sit still. "Oh, Karen, what a story you're going to have! You came to write a simple haunted-house story, and look what's unfolding! Isn't this exciting?"

I exhaled shakily. "If people were mad at me before, they're really going to be mad now."

Ervin and Kimberly stayed so late, while we beat to death all the facts we knew, that I was exhausted by the time they left. With the violent deaths of the Saxons having been substantiated, I was able to think of nothing but my dream. What did my dream mean? Once again, as the hour grew late, I was running on overload. Each day in this town unraveled something worse than the day before.

And the storm, too, worsened. When we were alone again, Steve circled his arm around me. My head dropped onto his shoulder.

"You're tired, honey."

"I'm so tired I can barely keep my eyes open. It's emotion. Too much emotion. My whole body aches with fatigue."

"Let's get you back, then. You need to rest."

It was raining hard when we pulled out into the dark deserted street. The trees were blowing wildly. The thunder was not as loud as before, but it was still rumbling, and the rain pelted hard against the windshield.

Steve pulled up directly in front of my motel room and opened the car door.

"Please don't get out," I said. "There's no need for both of us to get soaked. I'll just run in quickly. Here, I've got the room key out."

"All right. I'll get in touch with you tomorrow."

"It was a lovely dinner, Steve. I like being with you."

"My sentiments exactly. Get some sleep now. God knows, you need it." He leaned over to kiss me lightly on the lips.

With rain pounding on my shoulders, I unlocked the outside door to my room. It wouldn't open more than a couple inches. I pushed it hard, then realized it was latched from the inside.

A second later, Steve was beside me. "What's the matter?"

"The inside chain lock is on! Someone must be in there." Fear rumbled inside me. The room was black and silent.

Steve knocked loudly, but the knocks failed to bring any response. "This is ridiculous!" he growled, then took my hand while we stormed off in the direction of the office.

It was one o'clock in the morning. Everything was dark, but the office door was open. Steve banged and shouted loud enough to be heard for a block, and at last Wanda's husband came out yawning. His shirt hung open.

"What's the matter out here? Trying to wake the dead? We're closed until 5:00 a.m." He yawned again. "Oh, Mayor Hayes! Didn't realize it was you. What's wrong?"

"One of your guests is locked out of her room. The door is latched shut."

The man looked at me, frowning. "Latched shut? I don't see how that's possible. Your name would be...?"

"Karen Barnett. Room 27." Steve and I were both soaked and shivering.

"Barnett. Let's see." He thumbed through the large book on the counter. "Barnett...our book shows you checked out this afternoon."

Chapter Nine

I was sure I hadn't heard right because the rain was pounding so hard on the roof and against the windows. "What did you say?"

"Checked out. That's what it says here."

"That's ridiculous! I haven't paid you and all my things are in the room."

"Bill's paid," the man said, rubbing his fingers over the stubble on his chin. "The room's been let to somebody else, after you checked out."

"Wanda was here when I left this afternoon! I took nothing with me. She knows perfectly well I didn't check out. In fact I told her I'd be here several days more."

"Sorry. Real sorry, ma'am. You must be mistaken. I'd give you another room, but we're full up."

"You haven't been full up in seven years," Steve snarled. "What the hell is going on?"

Clancy Clark would not look at him. "All I know is Miss Barnett checked out and another party checked in. I regret the misunderstanding—"

"Who do you think you're talking to? A couple of idiots? What happened to Karen's belongings? I'll have the law over here, Clancy! Hell, as far as you're concerned, I *am* the law. I want an—"

The elderly man looked at Steve with eyes so full of terror that Steve drew back, startled. Then, squinting, speaking barely above a whisper, he leaned over the counter. "Who instigated this, Clancy? You might as well tell me now, before I have you hauled to the police station in this storm."

"I don't . . . know."

"I strongly suggest that you remember."

"I don't know, I swear! Somebody called me, said they'd put me out of business if Miss Barnett was allowed to stay here. They meant it, too. I'm an old man with a weak heart, Mayor Hayes, not young like you. My fighting days are long gone."

Steve swore a terrible oath. "Somebody called you? What kind of voice?"

"A man's. Sort of muffled, but he sounded real mean. Said they were watching the motel and Karen Barnett better not be here after today."

I touched Steve's arm. "I'll go to the hotel in town, then. Mr. Clark, will you please give me my things?"

Without a word he turned, disappeared for a few moments, and returned with my two suitcases. I assumed Wanda had packed everything into them. I also assumed she was awake in the next room and didn't have the courage to face me, after telling me only hours ago that I was welcome here. The old couple had been badly frightened.

Rain was dripping from Steve's dark hair when he picked up my bags. "This issue is far from over," he promised Clancy Clark. "Somebody has got a mistaken notion about who's running this town."

When we were in the car again, Steve said, "It won't be any use trying to check into the hotel. Whoever called the Clarks will have made sure you can't get in there, either, and anyway, the hotel office doesn't stay open this late. They figured if you had no place to stay, you'd have to leave town."

"They picked a great night for it."

"What they underestimated is me. Whoever is behind this must assume that since you and I have just met, we're only acquaintances. That assumption is going to be their fatal mistake."

"Steve—" shivering, I tried to smooth back my wet hair "—I don't know what to do."

"You're staying with me, of course."

I was startled. "How will that look?"

"Who gives a damn how it looks?" He seemed to reconsider this, because he looked at me and said gently, "I have a guest room. Does it bother you how both of us sleeping under the same roof looks to the town?"

"No. It's not my town, it's yours."

"It's settled then. There's no choice anyway. Nobody runs anybody out of my town, and especially not somebody I care about."

These words spilled out of him quite easily, and yet they made me feel soft and fluttery inside. He simply meant he liked me and I was welcome in his home. I had no hesitation about staying with him. I'd never trusted anyone more than I trusted Steve Hayes, even though I knew so little about him. He had too much respect for me and for himself to try to take advantage of the situation.

Steve carried my bags from the garage directly to his guest room, and said, "I'm going to make some coffee for myself because I can't sleep when I'm this mad. Do you want some decaf, or would you rather just go to sleep?"

I smiled. "There's nothing like standing in a driving rain to wake a person up. And yeah, you're right, getting really angry wakes a person up like nothing else can. I'd love some hot coffee."

"Good. I'll be in the kitchen. The bathroom is just down the hall. Clean towels on the shelf. Let me know if you need anything."

Feeling like I'd been through a war, I dried my hair and changed into my white terry robe. Fifteen minutes later I was in the kitchen with Steve, who'd changed into dry jeans and a sweatshirt. The smell of coffee filled the room.

"It's unbelievable," I said.

At the counter slicing an apple, he turned around. "What is?"

"Everything. Just everything."

"Yeah. Everything. Including you. Especially you. You show up one day and the world turns upside down. This town will never be the same."

"I'm ... sorry."

He laughed, set down the apple, picked me up at my waist and twirled me in the air as effortlessly as if I were a child. "Don't be sorry! This stagnant town needs airing out! I've always thought there was something weird about my grandmother keeping that haunted house. The place is full of ghosts, all right. I think it's time you and I had a talk with Daphne."

"Me?"

"Don't you want to meet my grandmother?"

"Yes, actually I do. I'd like to very much."

"Good. We'll go see her tomorrow." He poured out two cups of coffee.

I blew on the steam. "Steve, those three photos on the dresser in your guest room. Your family?"

"Yeah, my dad and my mother. The sullen little kid is me."

"Do you remember your father?"

"Just barely. I have one memory of him bringing home a dog for me."

"Your mother never remarried?"

"No. I had an uncle for a role model. Uncle Joe, my mother's brother. Daphne never could stand him because he spent his life working for somebody else, but Joe is a good guy. Heart of gold. I still spend every Thanksgiving with him, in spite of Daphne's protests and disparaging remarks."

"Sounds as though your grandmother is a snob."

"The worst. But at least she isn't two-faced. She is what she is and admits it, and I admire her for that. I should warn you, she's jealous of women I keep company with. Sees them as potential rivals."

"Good heavens, Steve! I've heard of possessive mothers, but grandmothers?"

"She plays the mother role. Sometimes she actually confuses me with my dad. I don't mean to paint her too harshly, Karen. I think you'll like her. The two of you have something in common—spunk."

The events of the past two days were taking their toll on me. I felt myself becoming shaky and weak, from fatigue and fear and frustration.

His arm circled my shoulders. "You're trembling. Are you okay?"

"Sure. I'm just tired."

"Instead of sitting here jabbering about my offbeat family, I ought to be comforting you."

"The sound of your voice is comforting. Just being with you helps more than you know."

"One wouldn't guess it from the way you're trembling."

"I think I need to go to bed." I yawned.

"Is it okay if I come in and kiss you good-night?"

"Sure."

The rain was pounding on the roof and against the window when I crawled between the crisp sheets in the guest room. Everything seemed illusory to me—the storm, this room, the night.

When I closed my eyes, the picture of the house on Sycamore swam before me. My heartbeat quickened and I forced my eyes open. Oh God, not that dream! Not now! Not anymore! I was too exhausted to fight off sleep for long, but the threat of dreaming frightened me.

Steve stood in the doorway of the guest room, his large frame silhouetted against the dim light of the hall. "You asleep?"

"No. I'm waiting for that promised good-night kiss."

The bed sagged with his weight. I could feel the warmth of his hands on my shoulders through my thin pajama top. He whispered, "Karen, are you cold?"

"No. Just..." My voice faded. I wanted more than anything in the world just for him to hold me. I didn't even know where the need was coming from; I knew only that it was there, and almost uncontrollable in its intensity. When Steve bent to kiss me good-night, I clung to him, wanting his strength to melt into me and become part of me. I fought back tears.

"It's okay," he whispered. "It's the dream that scares you, isn't it? And now, so close to the house, the dream is close again."

"Yes. I dreamed that murder. I keep trying to recall more of the dream, but I've suppressed it so long it's...so vague. If I were to dream it again, maybe I could remember, but...oh, I just can't bear it—"

His lips interrupted me. He held me close and prolonged the kiss. It was a kiss more tender than passionate.

"Karen, nothing can hurt you as long as I'm here. Not even that damned dream. I'll stay right here. I'll be with you, and you'll know I'm here, even while you sleep."

He urged me down onto the pillow and pulled the sheet and light blanket over me. Then he lay down beside me on the outside of the blanket. He adjusted the other pillow under his head and wrapped his arm around me.

"Steve," I whispered, "you're babying me."

"Damn right. You need me right now. Anything wrong with that?"

I was glad he couldn't see the mist form in my eyes. "No," I admitted, "there isn't anything wrong with that."

Even through the light blanket and sheet, I felt the warmth of his body. I felt the comfort of him seep all through me. *I do need you,* I thought as I was moving down into troubled sleep. *What would I do if you weren't here?* I had forgotten what it felt like to need a man. It didn't feel as bad to need someone as I thought it would. After all, this need and this man were temporary.

I drifted. The events of the day refused to leave me. I saw the stairway, waving in shadows like a snake. Shadows against the wall. A thudding noise broke the shadows apart. And the hand was there ... that small white hand with the ring ... a sparkling ring of diamonds and rubies. The hand did not move, but another did ... another hand reaching down, lifting the ring from limp fingers. And the white hand lay still again....

Terror gripped me. Footsteps pounded above me, below me ... screams echoed from the walls ... screams....

I did not know who was screaming, but the screams filled my head to bursting.

The coiling stairway tried to swallow me...and there was blood spattered against a background of white...and the black shadows became red...became flames...and the screams that wouldn't stop became flames....

I sat up with a cry of anguish, my heart pounding against my ribs, my eyes wet with tears.

Steve was beside me. He shot into a sitting position, saying my name, only my name, as he wrapped me in his arms and held me. I trembled violently. He held me tighter against his chest.

It had been so real, so vivid. More real than Steve wiping the tears from my cheeks now with the sleeve of his sweatshirt. More real than the sound of his breathing. But gradually the world outside my dream was coming back.

"Steve..." I murmured. "The dream again. This time I saw fire...I saw the fire..."

"You didn't mention fire before."

"I don't remember seeing it. I've forgotten so much of the dream...because I tried to forget, but this time fire and...blood..." I shuddered and was unable to hold back a sob.

"Are you all right?"

"I will be in a minute."

He continued to hold me in silence. A light at the far end of the hallway cast a dim shadowy glow through the open door. Wind blew rain against the windows and the night seemed endless.

Presently he asked, "Can I get you anything?"

"No...thank you..."

I felt his warmth move away from me. He stood up, unzipped his jeans and kicked them off, then pulled his sweatshirt over his head. His body, clad only in briefs, was outlined in the dim light. He pulled the sheet and blanket aside and got in bed next to me, urging me gently back onto the pillow. Then he was snuggled against me in the dark, his arm resting on my waist.

"Don't worry," he said gently. "I'm here."

Somewhere in the night I was aware of Steve's breathing. My sleep was shallow because I tried to keep above the depth of dreams. I would stir and feel him with me and hear his breathing as he slept.

PALE WATERY LIGHT glowed from behind the bedroom curtains. I awoke with Steve's arms still around me. He was sleeping soundly now, as the summer morning's first bird songs were beginning to blend with the whimper of a dove. On his side, uncovered to the waist, he lay facing me, breathing softly, his lips slightly parted. As light of the new day filtered in, I could see the shadows of his eyelashes. I watched him sleep, enchanted by the beauty of him.

My body felt fatigued; I didn't want to move. I lay for a long time watching Steve sleep and trying to understand my feelings for him. I felt love. That word I'd been so afraid of for so long came easily now. I felt a deepening love for the man who had held me through the night. And this was scary. I didn't want to love him. There could be no future with him. I lived in a busy city with a thriving business of my own. He lived in a wicked haunted little town in the middle of the American prairies. He'd been clear, more than once, about the fact that he had no interest in marriage, and he meant it.

And yet I was falling in love with him. It wasn't the usual kind of falling in love, with all the erratic emotions and doubts and agonies. It was so strangely calm, so strangely right. I felt as if I had always known the man who was sleeping beside me, had always loved him.

He began to stir. His eyes didn't open but his hand moved over me softly—over my back and down over my hips. I reached out and touched his face tenderly, my fingertips along his cheek, unsure if he was actually awake.

When I kissed his closed eyelids, a small sound of contentment caught in his throat and he drew me closer. His hand began to caress me with tender yearning. I welcomed his yearning and no longer wanted to deny my own. I slid my hands over the expanse of his chest, down to the waist of his briefs, and trembled with wanting him.

He guided my hand, in response, his way of telling me without words that he wanted, too. . . .

"I didn't plan this," he whispered.

"I know."

"Karen—are you sure?"

I'm sure I love you. I'm sure I can't help loving you. . . . The words echoed in my head, but I couldn't say them aloud. I answered only with a nod as his lips drew close to mine.

I drowned in his kiss. Everything was whirling and swirling around me and inside me. Openmouthed, hungry, the kiss was fuel to the flames of my need. I felt the caress of his hands on my skin, felt the fabric of my pajamas slide away. Time disappeared. The whole world shrank.

He whispered, "I want you so badly I can't stand it."

"I feel the same."

Grasping his hands I tried to hold myself on earth, but he was soaring somewhere and taking me with him. Somehow when our bodies merged our souls connected, bonded in a split second as bright as if every sun in the universe had slammed together into one great explosion of light. That instant I knew my world would never be the same again.

STEVE LIKED summer mornings. He fixed breakfast—coffee and juice and cold cereal—and took it to the shaded table in his back yard, as he did, he said, every morning when the weather was good. Birds sang from the branches above us as we ate.

"Your back yard is lovely," I said.

"I don't go in for gardening, except for keeping the grass mowed. The flowers along the fence were here long before I came."

"Hollyhocks. I haven't seen hollyhocks in such a long time. Did you ever make hollyhock dolls when you were a kid?"

He looked at me strangely, nodded, got up from the table and went into the house. A few seconds later he was back with a box of toothpicks.

"What fun!" I said, and almost ran to the fence where the tall flowers grew in profusion.

"Pink for the skirt," I said, "and white buds for the head and the hands. And here—" I picked two fat lavender buds "—are the pants for yours."

"How did you know I wanted purple pants?"

I hesitated. "Don't you?"

"Yeah. These guys are in the French court. They always had purple pants."

"This isn't purple. It's lavender."

"Same thing."

I laughed and saw no need to argue about the color, while I watched him take a third bud for the body, impale it on first one toothpick, then another, at an angle, and slide on the smaller buds for pant legs. "They *do* look like courtly bloomers," I said.

"He's the Scarlet Pimpernel. Where's his lady?"

"Here, getting ready." The upside-down flower formed a full skirt of pink. I gave her puffy sleeves of white buds and a head of another bud while Steve supplied his Scarlet Pimpernel with a lavender head.

"I'd forgotten about hollyhock dolls," he said, holding his up for inspection. "I've looked at hollyhocks a million times and never remembered. Now suddenly it all came back."

He handed me the Scarlet Pimpernel. Then, lost in wonderful memories of childhood, I made the flower dolls dance over the tabletop. Steve watched in fascinated silence.

It wasn't until I tired of playing with the flower dolls that he said, "I'm going to phone my grandmother and tell her we're coming over to see her."

"But it's early."

"Ten o'clock is early?"

"Ten o'clock? You're kidding!"

"Time got away from us this morning."

A warmth coursed through me at the memory of our time together. "Do you have to be at work?"

"My schedule is my own." He cocked his head and studied me. "You look beautiful this morning."

I smiled. I was wearing a pale pink summer dress with a subdued floral pattern of white and mint green, and pearl earrings. "Your grandmother wasn't friendly when I spoke to her on the phone about getting into the house. Are you going to tell her you took me inside?"

"I've been trying to figure out what to tell her. Dealing with Daphne can be a tricky business. It might be best to talk about the rumors and not tell her why you wanted to go in there. If she asks, of course, we'll have to tell her the truth. The important thing is to learn what we can about the Saxons and the ghost.''

''She might have heard about my asking questions.''

''Yeah, she probably has. Nothing gets by her.'' He rose. ''We'll take our chances.''

I felt apprehensive as we walked down the shady sidewalk that morning. Our destination was only four short blocks away, so small was the elite residential area of Tyrone.

As we passed the Saxon house, I stopped to gaze up at the great old building. ''It's so silent. If only that house could talk. No one has ever gone ghost hunting?''

''Not to my knowledge. You and I saw nothing.''

''Maybe that's because it was daytime.''

He shrugged.

We hadn't intended to be distracted by the empty house this morning, but its mysteries tugged at us. We found ourselves wandering around the grounds. A squirrel jumped from the roof onto the thick branch that supported the tree house.

''Being here gives me strange feelings,'' I said. ''Even watching that squirrel run along the tree house . . .''

In what had been a flower bed at the side of the house, close to the steps of the back porch, I spotted a small pile of carefully arranged stones and paused. ''Children must have done this. It looks like a pet's grave.''

''A pet or a wild animal. A dead squirrel, or maybe . . .''

''A rabbit,'' I finished.

''Yeah, a rabbit. A baby rabbit.''

I stared up at him. ''You lived next door. This could have been your work, couldn't it? Maybe you . . . somehow remember . . .''

"I don't know. I was too young to remember. Nothing about living there comes back. How did *you* know it was a rabbit?"

"Maybe it isn't."

"We both know it is."

"How could we?"

"You're right, we couldn't." He looked up at the silent house. "I suppose you want to go in there again."

"I want very much to, but not when we'd have to hurry. Not this morning, with your grandmother expecting us."

As we walked, with Skipper Flash following close behind, I thought about the grave of the rabbit. It could have been any of a hundred things, but Steve and I both believed children had buried a small wild rabbit there. I thought about the hollyhock dolls we had made in Steve's back yard. I thought about the river and romping on the river islands, and drinking from his hands. Children's play. It was easy to be a child with Steve.

Daphne Hayes's house was the largest home in Tyrone. It sat on a rise at the end of Maple Street, back from the sidewalk, with a great expanse of front lawn and a circular drive. Its windows were long and narrow, several on the first story, but fewer windows on the second and third. With its gables and its ugly windows, the house looked sinister. It had never been lovely, as the house on Sycamore in its heyday had been.

The closer we came, the more unease swelled within me. Foreboding. I tried to tell myself the discomfort was only because of my phone conversation with Steve's grandmother. Her unfriendliness. That was unfair, though, I rationalized, because she'd had no idea whom she was talking to. I was going there now as Steve's friend. There was no reason for my dread; still it persisted. That enormous austere house didn't help.

Steve took my arm on the steps. I was grateful he couldn't hear my heart pounding. The door was opened by a middle-aged woman dressed in dark slacks and a white blouse. Steve introduced her as Daphne's housekeeper. She seemed happy to see Steve, while she glanced suspiciously in my direction as if it were up to her to decide whether or not I was worthy of the old lady's company.

"Your grandmother is in the sitting room," she said.

There was a coldness in this house. Many of the draperies were drawn, so it was darker than it needed to be on this bright day. Steve led me down a short hallway.

Daphne Hayes, dressed in a belted, dark velvet skirt and lacy beige blouse, rose graciously to her feet as we entered, and extended her arms to Steve. She looked all of her seventy years, but her movements were agile. Her face was wrinkled, her hair white and worn in a bun at the back of her neck, and the pearls Kimberly had described hung low at her neck. Her grandson gave her a swift hug, then turned to me. "Daphne, this is Karen Barnett, from Los Angeles."

The old woman reached a hand to me. "How do you do, Karen. Please sit down and tell me what brings you here. Would you like coffee or tea?"

"Coffee," Steve said. "You, Karen?"

"Yes, thank you."

It was impossible for me to relax in this room of dark velvet draperies and Chinese antique cabinets. The old woman would not meet my eyes, and this bothered me. The housekeeper ducked out to get the coffee. Daphne motioned us to the chairs.

"Karen," she began, "I apologize for being abrupt on the phone when you called. I didn't realize you were a friend of Steve's. People ask about the house, you know. They hear the stories of the ghost, and they're curious."

"I understand," I said.

"I presume Steve has let you inside by now. I know he has a key."

"Yeah," he said with an amused grin. "We went in for a few minutes."

"And did you see the ghost?"

I tried to smile, but she was making me terribly uncomfortable. Her voice, her very presence, bothered me. "Not a sign of a ghost," I said.

"She's not an active ghost," Daphne said. "Shows herself only rarely."

"You've often told me the ghost was nonsense," Steve said.

"Of course it is."

Daphne, when she finally looked at me, looked at me with hostility. She didn't like the fact that I was here, prying into the history of the Saxon house.

Steve got right to the point. "Daphne, we know that the Saxons died violently. Wayne Saxon shot his wife and then himself. Why didn't you tell me they were dead when I asked you about them?"

The old woman squinted at her grandson. "Who on earth told you a thing like that?"

"We found the coroner's records. Police records have mysteriously disappeared. There's been a massive cover-up of this story for twenty-five years. Karen and I would like to know why."

Chapter Ten

Daphne Hayes grasped the pearl necklace at her neck and fell backward onto a chair. "Good heavens, Steve! That grizzly story! Why would anyone want to discuss anything so horrid?"

"It's a good juicy bit of gossip, Daphne. I can't see you or anybody else shrinking from it, unless there is more to the story. That's what I'd like to know. What's the rest?"

"My dear, isn't that enough?"

"Everybody I've approached about this has lied to me. Pretended not to remember. I find that damned curious. Tate McGil is the only person willing to talk about the Saxons—after Karen found their tombstones in the cemetery."

Her eyes grew wide. "Tate McGil? Why, that man wouldn't know the truth if he tripped on it."

"He was telling the truth about this. Which is more than I can say for you."

"Steve! I've never lied to you about anything in my life. All right, I omitted telling you about the Saxons. I knew those people, that poor woman. Mind, I knew her only slightly, but I respect the dignity of her memory. You know a town is a family and like all families we try to cover up our scandals. Don't make it sound so deceitful, Steve, dear. All we're doing is protecting our past."

"From whom?"

"From notoriety."

"From all subsequent generations, it seems to me."

"From further scandal. Once something is over, there is nothing to be gained by dredging it up." She looked pointedly at me. "I'm sure the history of murder in a haunted house would make excellent copy, Karen, dear. But it would bring curiosity seekers to Tyrone, and we wouldn't want that, would we? I certainly don't relish the idea of strangers snooping around my property setting up ghost watches."

"I can understand that," I said gently. "Is this concern about publicity the reason a so-called Citizens Auxiliary is trying to force me to leave?"

"Citizens what?" She turned to her grandson. "What is that?"

He gazed hard at her. "Someone using that name has been threatening Karen."

"Someone? Who?"

"I don't know who, but it has to do with her asking questions about the Saxons' deaths."

"I can't believe such a thing!"

I said, "Mrs. Hayes, I have no intention of writing an article about your house. My reasons for wanting to see it are personal. You see, I found a photo of the house among my mother's things after she died. I was curious because I had childhood dreams about the house, even though I've never been in Tyrone. I said I was a writer because I didn't know how else to explain my presence here. Whatever I learn is for my information only. I think my mother might have known the Saxons."

The old woman looked at me strangely. It was a hostile look, I thought at first, but then her expression softened. "I see..." she murmured, letting my words compute. "Well, this is quite a different matter, if you're not a writer. You dreamed about a photograph. Is that what you said?"

"I dreamed about the house. I found the photo only a few weeks ago, after my father died."

"Karen dreamed about a murder, too," Steve said.

Daphne sucked in her breath. "Oh, you poor dear! Do you think these people were relatives of yours? Perhaps you overheard your parents talking?"

"They couldn't be relatives or I'd know about them. Yes, it's possible my parents talked about it sometime, if they knew. The other possibility is that it's sheer coincidence my mother had that photo, and my dreams are psychic. But—"

"What did you dream?" she asked abruptly.

Her question threw me off guard. If the subject was so repugnant to Steve's grandmother, I was shocked she'd ask for details. But then, she probably remembered some details of the crime and was curious about the accuracy of my dreams. I wasn't inclined to put a frail old woman through my horror, though. Nor was I, in this ugly quiet house, in the mood for a discussion of my nightmares.

I said, "The dreams were vague and confusing. I didn't actually see anyone murdered. It was just the...feelings and the fear. A child's nightmare."

"There's a reason for those dreams," Steve said. "And we don't think they're psychic or based on coincidence. One way or another we're going to find out what they are."

His grandmother's head jerked up. "We?"

Steve gave her one of his imposing looks. "At first I just wanted to help Karen. It seemed very important to her. But now that we've uncovered a conspiracy, somebody is trying to scare her out of town. The Clarks who run the motel were threatened by retaliation if Karen was allowed to remain there."

"This happened in Tyrone? But we know everybody in town! No one would do such a thing, or have a reason to."

"Someone has a reason," he said. "And that's what we want to find out."

"Oh my!" Her hand was trembling on the pearls. "Karen, is it safe for you at the motel?"

"She's staying with me," Steve answered.

She shot him a look of grave disapproval. "Is that wise? People will talk!"

He laughed. "God forbid, Daphne. What would the good people of Tyrone gossip about if it weren't for me? It hasn't bothered me yet."

"It bothers me," she said softly.

Steve had been pacing the room. He stopped at the back of her chair and placed a hand on his grandmother's shoulder. "Come on, Daphne. You can't mean that. You're the one who taught me the worst thing that can happen to a Hayes is *not* to be talked about."

She smiled. "Karen might not be so thick-skinned. Nor am I, in my frail old age."

"Frail, my foot."

The housekeeper interrupted with a tray of coffee, which she left on the ornately carved, glass-topped Chinese chest that served as a coffee table. Steve automatically stepped forward to pour, obviously well trained by his grandmother. It was too dark in here. Large trees kept out some of the sunlight. The view through the window was a study in contrasts: a meadow was filled with trees and knee-high swamp grass and cattails. There must have been a natural spring that formed a marsh at the back of the house, cutting the property off from its rear neighbors.

I felt restless, out of place. Daphne's perfume was strong. I studied the patterns of the Oriental rug. I noted the piano that stood in one corner of the room and wondered if Daphne played it, or if Steve had when he lived here as a youth. I wondered how many times in his growing-up years Steve had crowned himself on the low-hanging crystal chandelier before he learned to automatically duck when he walked under it, as he did today.

Daphne held the saucer and cup daintily on her lap. "So, Steve, dear. You came here to grill me about what I know of those people and why I bought their house."

"Why did you buy it?"

"It wasn't one of my wiser investments, was it? Well, it was so cheap, a giveaway. I assumed I could repair the fire damage, paint it up a bit and sell it for a profit. But then the blessed ghost stories began, and it was no use. Nobody would live there and nobody would buy it."

"Why didn't you give it to the city?"

"The idiots didn't want it. They need a nursing home, but it has to be something on one floor. The house is too big, they said, far too expensive to renovate to meet their needs. Well, in all fairness, that's true. It is too big."

I set down my cup. "What do you know about the Saxon family, Mrs. Hayes?"

"No one knew the Saxons well. His wife was much younger then he, I do remember that." She sipped her coffee slowly. "They came from a small town near Omaha and bought the sporting-goods shop after old man Danson died. They bought the house from Danson's heirs, too. They never got involved in community affairs. What can I tell you? No one had any idea why the man . . . did what he did."

"There must have been gossip as to why."

"Oh, gossip, yes. She was half his age and very pretty, and people speculated about another man. But there was never anything proved. No one knew a thing. And how could we, really? I mean, how could anyone know what went on in their private lives? They were found dead that awful day and their secrets died with them."

"Were they alone in the house when it happened?"

"Yes. They were found by police after a neighbor heard screams and gunshots. I'm glad your mother wasn't home that morning, Steve. She might have rushed in on the grizzly scene."

"Where was I?"

"In preschool."

"I don't recall anything."

"Of course not. The authorities were very careful not to frighten any of the neighborhood children. They were very good at keeping the investigation quiet so as to cause as little stir as possible."

"The children are grown now." He scowled. "And no police files exist, and half the town has amnesia. That's a little too damned quiet, don't you think?"

"Don't swear, dear. You weren't raised to talk like that."

Steve burst into laughter. "Daphne, you're too much. Now, come on! What else do you know about that murder?"

"Me? How could I know anything about it? How could anyone? As I recall, Wayne Saxon set a gasoline fire, presumably with the intention of burning down the house after..." She shivered. "I don't know and never wanted to."

"What became of the Saxon's child?" I asked.

The old woman's pale blue eyes narrowed and became stone cold.

"I assume relatives took the children...."

"Children? They had more than one?"

She blinked several times. "I think there were two."

"Did they have a girl?" Steve asked.

His grandmother nodded. Her thoughts seemed far away, as if she were trying to remember.

"Were there any relatives in Tyrone?"

"No, I'm sure not."

Steve set down his cup. "Karen, you could be connected with that family."

"Are you thinking I might be that girl? No. I wasn't adopted."

"Are you sure?"

"Of course I'm sure."

"She could hardly be old enough," Daphne Hayes said. "This all happened some twenty-five years ago, and the girl was ten."

I remembered a couple of baby pictures of me in a family album—one as a tiny infant in my mother's arms. Another at about age two, again with my mother. "No, I wasn't adopted," I assured them, while in one little corner of my brain, the idea sprang to mind that Steve was the one connected to the Saxon family—that it was his identity that was being protected. I had no reason for believing it except for the fact that somebody was obviously being protected and the list of possibilities wasn't very long. But then, Steve had baby pictures with his family, too.

Daphne said there were two children. It had to be true. She'd been in the town years. And she was still sharp, mighty sharp for a woman her age.

Steve hadn't touched his coffee. "Daphne, something else happened in the Saxon house that Sheriff Dyer is still covering up."

"Something else? Isn't two violent deaths enough?"

"Not enough to explain the runaround Karen and I have been getting. I think somebody else was there."

"You mean a witness?"

"I don't know. Maybe a child."

"Oh! How awful! Why would you think such a thing?"

"Karen's dream. What is Dyer hiding, Daphne?"

"I can't tell you what I don't know. Why do you insist on picking on me?"

"For one thing, you're a chum of Chuck Dyer's."

"Chum? What kind of word is chum?"

"And Chuck has a memory lapse that proves he is too senile to hold public office any longer."

Steve's voice chilled me. It chilled his grandmother, too. Her eyebrows shot up. "What are you saying?"

"I'm replacing him with a law officer I can trust."

"Steve!"

He leaned closer. "I don't like being toyed with and given the runaround. Chuck knows that."

"It's an elected position."

"It hasn't been an elected position for the past fifty years. I'm promoting Deputy Eckles. He's proved his loyalty to me and to this town."

"You're a dictator!" she said softly, bitterly.

"I'm what this damn town wanted. I'm what they've got."

"This is terrible! Chuck has always been loyal to you, more than you know."

"If he was doing his job right, he'd talk to me. And he'd be able to explain what happened in that police investigation."

"It was thirty years ago!"

"Twenty-five."

"Steve, please," his grandmother pleaded. "Leave this thing alone."

"I can't. Karen wants more information, and so do I."

Daphne shot me a vicious look. I understood why; I was the one who had kicked up the dust from a den of sleeping snakes. I was the biggest trouble that had hit Tyrone in years. Just under the surface, the snakes had begun writhing all over the place.

WHEN WE WERE WALKING back to Steve's house, I said, "Your grandmother doesn't like me one bit."

He smiled. "I didn't expect her to like you because you're young and beautiful and you're with me. She tends to be jealous."

"I think she's angry about what I started."

"Maybe that, too. Don't worry about Daphne. She'll come around. She always does."

"You have an interesting relationship with your grandmother. She takes the role of boss, yet she's afraid to go against you."

He smiled. "She says I'm like my dad. I'm the only person on the planet she can't rule with an iron hand."

"You really are a dictator around here, aren't you?"

He shrugged. "Like I said, they got what they chose. Somebody has to take charge. I haven't got the time or the patience to sit around and argue with this do-nothing council."

"You'd really fire the sheriff?"

"It's as good as done. Daphne will tell him, so he can resign with dignity. He's too old for the job now, anyway."

"Remind me never to cross you."

"The issue here is honesty, Karen."

"I know." I looked up at him. "Steve, have you considered the possibility that maybe it wasn't a murder/suicide? That maybe some other person killed them both?"

"Sure I've thought of it. And I've wondered if robbery was the motive."

"You mean the diamond ring?"

"Yeah."

"The ring was only part of a dream!"

"It was no dream. You were there, Karen. I don't know how, but you were there. These are not just psychic ramblings."

I couldn't answer; I could barely breathe at the thought that he could be—must be—right. We walked in uncomfortable silence. Sprinklers were swooshing around us. Now and then the fragrance of flowers filled the air. Steve took my hand. "Damn, if you could just remember more."

"I've spent years trying to forget."

"But it's got to be there in your subconscious."

"The longer I stay here, as I told you before, the more 'flashes' I get. Like the fire. The fire was set by Wayne Saxon, the day they died, according to your grandmother. This is driving me crazy!"

"What if you underwent hypnosis?"

My breath caught. "I'd be terrified!"

"But it might give us some answers."

"At this point, I'd kill for answers."

He squeezed my hand. "There's a doctor in Evensen—the town I grew up in before I came to live with my grandmother after my mother died. He works with hypnosis. We could go there and give it a try. It's a forty-minute drive."

"Oh, Steve, I get cold chills just thinking about it."

"I'll be with you. I'll stay right with you."

I swallowed. "Can a person recall a dream under hypnosis?"

"I don't know. I doubt it. If you recall more details, it won't be a dream you're remembering. It will be the actual event."

"In other words, it will prove whether I was really there or not."

"Yeah. That's why you've got to do it. Karen, if you were there, then you might be able to recount the rest."

"But I was—would have been—a baby!"

"Twenty five years ago you were four or five years old."

"Oh, God. This is a worse nightmare than the original!"

He looked at his watch. "I've got a few things to clear up at my office. Shouldn't take more than an hour. Then we can drive to Evensen. I'll give Dr. Markson a call and tell him we need to get right in. Let's hope he has an opening. If not, hell, he'll just have to make one."

He picked up his step. I hurried to keep up with him. "I couldn't have been there! I just couldn't have been!"

We were nearing Steve's yard. The dog ran ahead of us, found his ball on the steps and raced back to put it at Steve's feet, wanting him to play. Steve tossed the ball high and fast; Skipper caught it in midair, his tail wagging furiously.

"I'll confess something," I said, as we started up the drive. "For a while I wondered if Saxon's son could be you."

"Me?"

"Think about it. Your mother left town soon after this happened. Do you have any memories of Tyrone before you left?"

"No, almost none."

"A rabbit's little grave? Purple hollyhock dolls? Horribly creepy feelings inside the Saxon house? Daphne and the others are hiding *something* from you."

"Not my identity, for God's sake, Karen. Everybody knows I'm a Hayes. It's crazy...everything...two children unaccounted for..."

"I knew you'd choose the purple for the Scarlet Pimpernel," I said. "I knew how to dance the dolls."

"So did I."

"As if they'd danced before."

"Yeah."

We stared at each other.

"And the river. When I drank from your hands, I was drinking from the past. That's why it threw us—that moment—isn't it? It was a moment from the past."

"It's too farfetched!" He howled. "We're getting hysterical. Okay, there were two kids, a girl and a boy, both unaccounted for, but..."

"A brother and sister," I said weakly.

He fell into a deadly silence.

"The rabbit's grave..." I muttered.

He howled in protest again. "We're losing our minds! Do you realize? We're losing our minds! I know who I am and you know who you are, so why are we doing this?"

My eyes had filled with tears. "Because... we don't know how else to interpret what happened at the river."

"You mean the... magic..."

We were both thinking of the river, but we were also thinking of this morning, when we were bonded in love.

He reached over to wipe a tear of frustration from my cheek. His voice came gently. "We're not brother and sister. It isn't possible."

"Can we be sure? There is some unspeakable secret, and I think your grandmother knows what it is."

"We'll find those two kids," he vowed. "If they're alive, we'll find them."

Inside his house, Steve telephoned the hypnotist in Evensen and persuaded the doctor that we had to have an immediate appointment. It was, he told him, an emergency.

Steve kissed me. "You're damned brave to submit to this."

"I'm not brave. I'm desperate."

"Do you want to wait here and relax for an hour while I take care of a few work obligations?"

"I'll be too restless waiting here. I'd rather walk around town, browse in some stores, keep moving."

"Let's go, then." His voice was edgy. We could deny the fears all we wanted, but they wouldn't entirely disappear until we had some answers.

Main Street's dips were still puddled with water from last night's heavy rain, but the sidewalks were well drained and perfectly dry. As I window-shopped, I kept looking sideways at people, wondering if any of them were part of the Citizens Auxiliary. I was sure a threat to somebody! Before long, I began to think I was being followed. Time started to drag.

I went into the drugstore and sat down at the counter and ordered a cola. No sooner had I been served than I heard a voice calling my name.

"Karen!"

I turned quickly. Glen Hadsell was hurrying to the counter. He set a package on the floor and slid onto the stool next to mine. Everyone in the store had heard him call to me.

"What's going on?" he asked.

"I'm waiting for Steve."

"Hmm. You two have hit it off so well the local ladies have gone into mourning. Tongues are wagging all over town."

"I'm sure they are." Wouldn't it be a monstrous joke, I thought, if someone wanted me out of here just because of the attentions from the eligible rogue in the mayor's office? I stirred the cola with my straw. "It doesn't take much to start tongues wagging in Tyrone, does it?"

"You're right, it don't. Especially where our mayor is concerned."

"Life in the limelight."

Glen laughed. "Such as it is."

"Is it just my imagination, or are you all a little overprotective of your head official?"

"You could say that."

"Steve doesn't seem to me to be a man who needs protection from anybody."

"Only from himself, maybe." He motioned to the boy behind the counter and ordered coffee.

I felt more intense dislike for this man than I had felt the night before last—and mistrust. Why, I wasn't sure, but I knew I didn't like the way he always made Steve out to be the rogue. It was probably jealousy on his part, but nevertheless it was insensitive. I sipped my cola while he poured sugar into his steaming coffee.

"That isn't quite accurate," he said at last, and I had to try to remember what it was he'd said. Oh yes, the sour crack about protecting Steve from himself. "It's Stevie's past that people want to protect."

A rumble of fear went through me. Could it be true, then, that he wasn't really a Hayes by blood? Although I felt myself go pale with the fear, I wasn't about to give this man the satisfaction of my curiosity. Instead I disguised it. "And does His Honor appreciate all the protective efforts?"

"I doubt it. Though it ain't all for him. It's for the town, too. I mean, we ain't exactly proud to be represented by an ex-con."

"A what?"

He glanced at me, then away. "Hell's jiggers, you didn't know, did you?"

"You know perfectly well I didn't!"

"And you staying at his house? I figured he had the decency to tell you under those circumstances."

It took every ounce of my self-control to cover my shock with that fire-hot word *ex-con* pulsing through my brain. "The only circumstances, Glen, are that the Clarks kicked me out of the motel."

"Are you serious? What'd you do, play your TV too loud?"

"There are certain people who are very nervous about me being in town."

"Nah, come on. This is a hospitable town. Kicked you out, huh? Cuz must be smoking like an old fire engine."

"I think so."

An ex-con? I couldn't get the word to compute with the man I knew. Steve had been in prison? For what?

And if these people were so ashamed of his past, why had they elected him mayor? Because other candidates were afraid to run against him?

Glen could be lying. But I didn't think so. I was remembering back to my first conversation with Kimberly at the library, and how horrified she'd been with the idea of my writing an article about Tyrone's mayor. Her reaction made sense now. There were things about Mayor Hayes this town didn't want the world to know about. I tried to picture Steve behind bars, and it was impossible. Who was he really? And what the devil had he done?

One thing was for sure—I wasn't going to ask cousin Glen. I looked at my watch and slid from the counter stool, grabbing my check.

"You didn't finish your drink," he said.

"I never do. Have to run. Steve will be waiting for me."

Hurrying in the direction of his office, I kept imagining eyes following me. My head was spinning. So it wasn't just the mystery of the Saxon house this town was guarding! It was also the secret of their highest official's unsavory past! How likely was it that the two mysteries were connected?

It was highly likely, dammit. Nevertheless, I trusted Steve. I had to trust him. He didn't know the secrets of the Saxon house. Yet he hadn't told me the truth about himself—if, indeed, what Glen said was the truth. Maybe it wasn't my imagination that told me people were afraid of Steve.

When I reached the steps of the town hall where Steve's office was located, he was coming down.

"Perfect timing," he said. "My car is parked in the back."

I fell into step beside him.

"Are you hungry, Karen?"

"No, not yet."

"Okay, we'll get a bite in Evensen. We'll be there in less than an hour."

I think it was because of the ordeal I was facing with hypnosis that I decided not to ask Steve point-blank if he had ever been in prison. I didn't have the stamina to discuss it right then. Lord knew I had enough to worry about. That matter would have to wait.

"You're quiet," Steve said as he drove. "I hope this isn't going to be too tough, Karen. You can always back out, you know."

"If I felt there was any alternative, I would. But what other recourse do we have?"

"I've been trying to come up with people recourses—somebody on that original investigation besides Dyer—but it's damn near impossible to learn anything."

I studied Steve's handsome profile as he drove. "I couldn't get to first base without you, could I? If I were on my own, I'd have hit a wall."

"It's a walled city, all right. A medieval walled city disguised as Twentieth-Century Smalltown USA."

"You seem quite happy living in Tyrone."

"Why not? My ancestors were the town founders. Hell, I own a good portion of the town, part of it inherited from my father, part of it I bought. Daphne will leave me her numerous properties. I guess you'd have to say this town and I belong together."

And yet, I thought, his mother took him away from here. Why would she move away?

The town of Evensen was on a flat plain, unlike Tyrone, which sat in a river valley. Evensen's buildings were more modern. A large grain elevator dominated the town. We passed a railroad yard on the way in.

"This is where you grew up?" I asked him.

"Until I was twelve and went back to Tyrone. Evensen is larger than Tyrone, but I never liked it here. There's no river."

"The river...Steve is it true that you became mayor in order to save the river from developers?"

"Guilty as charged. And the fact that I needed a job."

"But you're an attorney."

"The attorney business isn't booming in Tyrone."

My eyes fixed on his hands as he drove. I thought about how little I knew of this man of contradictions. I wondered if I'd ever know. One part of him wanted to be close to me; another part didn't want to be close to any woman. He had a reason for his bitterness toward women, and I'd probably never know that, either.

He looked at his watch. "Our appointment is at two-thirty, which gives us time to eat. There's a good Chinese buffet here. Would Chinese suit you?"

"It would suit me fine. Hot tea will help calm my nerves."

Just before two-thirty we pulled up in front of a house, close to the main business street, that had been converted into a doctor's office. I had never dreaded anything the way I dreaded an encounter with my own subconscious mind. I'd forgotten the details of my nightmares because they were too horrible to deal with, and now I was about to try to force them back from the darkness.

Dr. Markson met us at the door. His smile put me at ease at once. We were led into a small, old-fashioned parlor, where we sat in easy chairs and explained to him what our objective was. He asked whether I had ever submitted to hypnosis before and whether or not I believed the dream was based on an actual experience. To the last question I could only answer that I did not know.

Steve said very little; it wasn't his interview. But his presence was important to me. I needed his support. When Dr. Markson had the information he needed, he asked me to lie on the sofa, where he proceeded to put me into a state of deep relaxation. It was easier than I imagined it would be. Time went away for me. Everything disappeared around me but the pleasant voice of the man speaking to me, softly, confidently.

"We are going into your dream," he said finally, after a long time of floating.

Trusting the hypnotist, trusting myself at his direction, I allowed the dream to come forward. The exterior of the house appeared first, with shadows of the trees moving over its face. Then the carved staircase, deep in shadow, with light showing at the bottom. I was looking down the stairs, and at the bottom, in a shaft of light, was the white lifeless hand. I could not see to whom the hand belonged because of the angle of the stairs, but I could tell it was a woman's.

Then I saw another hand reaching down and removing a ring from a finger of the still hand, tugging once or twice until the ring came loose. That ring...rubies and diamonds in platinum; I could see it clearly.

Screams around me. They seemed to be mine. But not all were mine. I descended the stairs in utter terror, coming closer and closer to the ringless hand. There were shouts around me now, frantic shouts. I heard my name. I heard a voice saying not to go down, saying it over and over, but I couldn't tell where the voice was coming from. I stood frozen, afraid to go any farther down the steps and afraid to go back up. My hands clutched the railing.

The screams were around me; I'm sure some were coming from me. My knees were trembling. I felt ice-cold.

I was aware of the cracking and sucking of flames but I could not see them nor feel the heat of them. The landing seemed to be rising to meet me.

I saw blood. A great pool of blood near the lifeless hand. But more. In the blood... footprints! At the edge of the pooling blood were the clear bright red prints of bare feet.

Chapter Eleven

Footprints in blood...bare feet...the bare feet of a child! I caught just a glimpse of another child...a boy. Were they his footprints or mine? I couldn't tell. Were they his screams or mine? I couldn't tell. I could barely see his face in shadow because he was running in the direction of the blue room on the first floor—the room of many windows. Then I saw flames coming from the direction in which the boy had run. I didn't know whether he had run into the fire or away from it.

With a kind of shock I felt his hand pulling mine...his hands—the child's—and I...I was a child, too. For the first time I had a sense of identity, at least enough to know that I was a child. He was pulling at me and I started running, but there was only one set of footprints in the blood....

Sobbing uncontrollably, I awoke to the gentle sound of Dr. Markson's voice. For an instant or two the room spun and I didn't know where I was, but then I was back in the quiet parlor and Steve was beside me, and the dream was gone.

A heavy silence fell over the room. Finally Steve said, "The boy in your dream? Who was he?"

I was wiping the tears from my face. "You know about him?"

"You described everything out loud—at Dr. Markson's urging."

"Thank heaven! Now I don't have to repeat it. I have no idea who he was. I don't even know who *I* was! What does the dream mean?"

"It is impossible to know whether the happenings in the dream were actual or symbolic," the doctor said softly. "All dreams are symbolic. The things you saw may have merely represented extreme childhood fears."

"The setting of the dream is real."

"Yes, we've established that. There's little question in my mind that when you were a child you saw something very, very frightening, so frightening that through the years it has gnawed away at you. However, dreams, particularly a child's dreams, can be very distorted. There is no way to judge the accuracy of this memory."

"Then it is a memory?"

"Something is. As I said, the process of dreaming may have distorted it. And again, it may not have. Let me qualify my last statement." Dr. Markson looked up over the rim of his half-glasses and set down the pen he had been using to furiously scribble. "I will say the only way to judge the accuracy of this memory is to obtain a description of the actual events that took place."

"We've been trying like crazy to do that," Steve said. "There are too many people trying to block us."

"The boy?" I asked, shaking the awful images from my head. "Who was he? I couldn't see his face...."

"The boy could have symbolized something," the doctor said. "The Jungian theory is that each part of a dream symbolizes something in ourselves. He might not have been a boy at all."

I shook this off. "The dream is old and real. It's been with me forever. The boy is real...he's been with me forever, too...I just didn't remember...until I saw the footprints in blood again...the boy was real...who was he?"

Steve knelt beside me. "Are you all right?"

The images would not leave me. I knew they never would. "Was he the Saxons' son? He must have been. But we know of three boys...don't we? The Saxons' son...and you, Steve...and Glen...your cousin... three...different boys—"

"Karen!"

I stared at him glassily. "Who was he?"

"Glen? Me? Why the devil would you come up with our names?"

"I'm grasping, I guess. Steve, that house was...was full of children! The screams were not those of adults, I'm sure of it!"

Dr. Markson said, "It's highly unlikely a man would shoot his wife and himself in a house full of children."

"I know," I conceded. "I know." What I was remembering, though, was Steve's fear of that house. And Glen Hadsell's odd behavior about it. And Daphne's revelation that there were two Saxon children, one of them a girl.

What I had feared most—seeing a body attached to the lifeless hand—I hadn't seen. But of course the hands were there like always...hands...and that sparkling ring.

ON THE DRIVE BACK to Tyrone, I realized how much the hypnosis had taken out of me. The late-afternoon sun heating the car and the drone of the engine, and the motion, made me sleepy. I nodded off several times in the frustration of reliving the vivid pictures of the dream.

Those small bare, red footprints...running... Was the boy the Saxons' son? And who was I? What was I doing there? And why did the boy come running to or from the flames of the fire? Why had he run through blood? Or why had I? One of us had!

Thinking back, I felt there was another presence above me on the stairwell. Someone above, someone below, a shadow running past. In the car, I relived it all again, straining to remember.

I mumbled, "Steve, it was horrible."

He put his hand on my knee. "You were terrified. I don't buy Dr. Markson's Jungian symbolism stuff. Your description of the house itself was too vivid—and accurate."

"I didn't buy it, either." I sat back exhausted, asking myself over and over, *Who were they? Who were they?*

So involved was I with the children of the dream, I found no strength left to put to Steve the other question that haunted me. Was he really an ex-convict, or was it Glen's despicable idea of a joke? That afternoon, I didn't even want to know.

My car was still parked at the Country Inn Motel. Steve stopped there so I could pick it up. Then he drove to his office to get his messages and make some calls, and I managed somehow, in my shaky state, to drive back to Steve's house.

On Sycamore Street, the big haunted house looked the same—but not quite. It stood in stately sinister silence, guarding its hideous secrets behind locked doors and boarded windows. I stopped along the curb to stare at it.

Sitting in my car, I hadn't noticed the two women walking along the sidewalk. When they were within just a few feet, one of them turned and saw me. Terror distorted the features of her face. "You!" she shrieked.

"The ghost!" Her voice trembled. She staggered and almost fell.

My heart lurched with fright. "What? What are you talking about?"

The distraught woman did not answer me, as if I did not exist. Instead she raved to her friend, "I saw her at the window. It was her! Her...the ghost!"

Her friend looked at me, embarrassed and nervous. "Stella saw the ghost," she affirmed hesitantly.

"Clear she was..." the swooning woman insisted. "Last night the high window lit up and I saw her from my back porch! It was her...you..."

"I'm not a ghost!" I said, anger trembling in my voice. "I don't know what the devil you think you saw, but it wasn't me."

"It was! It was your face in the window! Your face!"

By this time, I was shaking as much as she was. I saw no point in trying to argue with a madwoman, but perhaps she wasn't mad, only frightened. Frightened of my face. This living nightmare was getting worse! Now *I* was the ghost?

I drove on to Steve's house without seeing the road, or seeing anything but the look on that woman's face when she'd seen me. Skipper came running out to meet me when I pulled into the driveway, and he followed me through the unlocked back door into the house.

I knelt to hug him, clinging to the warmth and strength of him. "Skipper, you're the only thing that's real! Even your master is full of dark secrets. Your neighbors are crazy. Your town is filled with shadows that are getting colder and more evil by the hour. You alone, sweet old guy, are who you appear to be."

The dog responded with wild affection, thumping his tail and licking my face. When I released him, he ran up to the den to find his ball, then brought it down. I threw it in the air a few times. Skip never let the ball reach the floor.

As I busied myself in Steve's kitchen, clearing up the breakfast dishes we had left, images swam before my eyes. Images of those small footprints in blood. Images of the fear on the face of a woman at the sight of me. Images of Steve with the shadows of cell bars on his face....

Skipper stayed near me, as if he knew I needed his presence. I found lettuce in the refrigerator and remembered a tomato plant in the back yard with one red ripe tomato on it. I would busy myself making a salad.

I was washing the vegetables when Steve came in, talking to the dog, who had run to the back door to greet him.

"I didn't expect you this soon," I said.

"What are you doing? Cooking?"

"You have salad and hamburger. I thought I'd start dinner."

"Great! We'll grill the hamburgers outside." He kissed me on the cheek.

I thought what a domestic scene this was—Steve coming home for dinner, petting the dog, kissing me on the cheek while I stood at the kitchen counter. *Things are never what they seem,* Glen had said. He was right.

Steve said, "I have news."

"So do I."

He leaned against the counter, facing me, his arms around my waist. "You first."

"This damn town of yours is bewitched! I stopped my car in front of the Saxon house on the way home. Two women were walking by. One of them started shrieking that I was the ghost. Can you believe it? She went pale as

chalk and almost fainted. She was raving that she had
seen the ghost at the window last night, and it had my
face. Honestly, I don't know how much more craziness I
can take."

Steve's mouth gaped open. "What did she look like?"

"Fiftyish, curly gray hair, short, bright crimson lip-
stick."

"Stella Barrow. They live in the house next door, the
one I was born in. I've never known Stella to be hysterical."

"She was today."

"It must be part of this conspiracy to scare you away."

"I thought of that. But she was genuinely frightened.
She wasn't faking her fright when she saw me."

"Weird." He drew me toward him. "Very weird!"

"You said you had news. I hope it's better than mine."

"It is. Erv Eckles got me a list of law officers who
worked for the city at the time of the Saxon deaths. One
of them, Henry Paulson, is still around. He's been retired for years; in fact I didn't realize he was an ex-
policeman. I phoned him. He hesitated at first, but since
he couldn't find any logical reason for refusing he agreed
to talk to me. Something changed in his voice as soon as
he agreed. I can't define it, but there was something
there—an odd kind of eagerness, an excitement, barely
disguised."

"Did you tell him you wanted to discuss the Saxon
case?"

"I didn't have to. He knew."

"But if he knows what happened, he's one of them—
the keepers of the secret and the perpetrators of the cover-
up. Do you want me to go with you?"

"I've been trying to decide. Henry agreed to see me in
the morning. I don't know whether he'd clam up when he

saw you, or whether we should level with him about . . . you."

"I'm an outsider, Steve. I'm the stirrer of the hornets' nest. I think you'd have a better chance of getting information if you talked to him alone."

"You're probably right."

He opened the refrigerator. "Want a beer?"

"Sure."

"I wonder if we should talk to Stella Barrow," he said, flipping the top of a can open and handing it to me.

"We'd have to take a paramedic with us. She's convinced she saw me as a ghost. What else could she tell us?"

"I guess we should give her time to calm down."

Steve took a sack of potato chips from the counter and sat down at the table, munching chips and swallowing the beer, and obviously in no hurry to eat.

"It's still too hot to light the barbecue. Besides, I want to talk some more about your dream."

I didn't. I wanted to talk about Steve's past, but it hadn't been easy deciding how to approach the subject.

"Steve," I began, reaching for a chip, "where did you go to college?"

"The University of Nebraska, in Lincoln. Where did you go?"

"Montana University. I was just wondering—"

The telephone rang. He reached around behind him to answer it.

"Yeah?" He sat up suddenly with interest. "Yeah!"

Skipper started to bark at something he heard in the front. I let him into the back yard so the barking wouldn't disturb Steve. As soon as he was outside, the dog began jumping up on the side gate, still barking. I looked out along the side of the house and saw nothing. Someone, or maybe another dog or a cat, had probably gone by the house. I left the Chesapeake snarling at the gate and went back inside.

Steve was hanging up the phone. "That was Henry Paulson. He said his wife is at a church meeting and asked if I could come now, while she's gone, instead of in the morning. What's Skipper carrying on about?"

"He started barking for no apparent reason. You're going now, then?"

He rose from the table, swallowing beer. "Henry asked if I was coming alone and I answered yes, but he said if I didn't come alone, it was no problem as far as he was concerned."

"Really? Do you think he meant me?"

"Sure. He's heard the jungle drums. This is interesting as hell. I think Henry is going to crack the dam, Karen, and I think he's anxious to do it."

"I hate to sound so suspicious of everybody, but could it be a setup?"

"It could, but I can't believe whoever wants you out of town would try anything funny with me."

I went into the guest room to get my purse. Steve was in the back yard patting the dog when I came back. Skipper was still very distracted, growling low in his throat and running to the gate and back.

"What's the matter with you?" his master asked. When he unlatched the gate, the dog tore around to the driveway and began jumping up on the door of my car.

Steve was right behind him. "Hey, you old fool, stop that! You're scratching the paint!"

"Is he afraid he'll get left behind when we leave?" I asked, catching up with them.

"He's never done this before." In spite of Steve's scolding, the dog jumped up on the car door again.

"What the hell is wrong with you?" Steve opened the door and stopped short. He swore.

On the car seat lay a clay figure wrapped in a piece of torn white cloth with red stains, like blood. Three straight pins were stuck in the heart of the figure and two more were in its right arm. A voodoo doll! I stepped back in shock.

Steve reached in and picked it up. "Child's soft clay," he said. "This is unbelievable!"

"Someone must have thrown it into my car just a few minutes ago, when Skipper started barking."

Steve stood staring at the thing, his thoughts so far away he hadn't even heard me. "I've seen one of these before," he muttered. "Once a long time ago. But I can't think where."

My stomach turned; I didn't want to touch it. The figure had what looked like real hair—light brown, the color of my hair—and the stains on the cloth were most certainly blood. "Voodoo, Steve? Who in Tyrone dabbles in voodoo?"

"I don't know. This isn't kids' play. It's meant as a serious threat."

For the first time Steve and I both realized my life was in danger. Livid, muttering, he crushed the humanlike clay figure in his hand till it formed a ball.

"Be careful! You'll run those pins through your hand!"

He looked up at me. "You don't believe in this stuff, do you?"

"No. If I did, I'd be terrified. I'm scared enough already."

Steve started to fling the clay ball at the garbage can, but realizing Skip would jump for it, he walked over and flung it furiously against the inside of the can and banged the lid. His hand was bleeding from the pins.

"I'm not going to let you out of my sight!" he declared, then strode to my car. He rolled up the windows, locked both doors and reached into his pocket for his keys. "Come on, I'll drive."

In his car, he slammed his palm against the steering wheel before he started the engine. "Damn! It's madness! Where have I seen a voodoo doll? I remember seeing one once with straight dark hair stuck on the clay, and a red cloth tied with a piece of brown string. Pins in the heart. I remember the doll, but it was so long ago I can't remember *where* I saw it...." His voice trailed off. "If I could just remember." Leaning back against the seat, he closed his eyes. "It was a long time ago. I think I might have been with my cousin."

"Glen?" I sat forward. "Could it be Glen who did this? I know he doesn't like me."

"He doesn't like me, either, but I don't think this is his style."

"I'm not so sure," I muttered, remembering with a sickening start what Glen had told me earlier today about Steve. Could his motive for telling me Steve was an ex-convict have been another attempt at getting me to leave?

Desperately I wanted to confront Steve with Glen's accusation. Desperately. But once again, it was not the time. We were on our way to Henry Paulson's, and what this man remembered about the Saxon deaths could put a light on the mystery, if he was willing to talk. I sighed shakily and tried to control my emotions.

Steve put his hand on my knee. "Are you all right, Karen?"

"I'm shaking."

"Frankly, I don't know how you're holding together after all that's happened in the last few hours, capped off with Stella Barrow and now this sick threat. You're made of stern stuff. Do you think you've got the stamina to talk to Henry?"

You skipped the part about my discovering your secret past, I thought, and didn't say it. "If Henry knows why the Saxons died, it would take more stamina to try to sit on my curiosity, waiting, than to get over there and find out what he knows."

"Good. That's how I feel." He started the engine.

"What are we going to tell him about me?"

"I thought we'd try the truth."

"Do we dare?"

"Maybe he knows already."

The streets narrowed. Houses became smaller as we swung around to the northwest of town, near the railroad. Steve pulled up in front of a small house with siding painted green on the bottom half and white on the upper. The house was old, but well-maintained, and was fronted by a smooth green lawn. The neighboring homes and yards were not as well kept; the neighborhood was somewhat rundown.

Henry Paulson was waiting for us. He was standing in the yard as Steve pulled into the drive. "If you wouldn't mind, would you park in the garage? I'd just as soon nobody saw your car here."

Steve pulled inside, and Paulson closed the door behind him. He greeted me and led us through a door that opened into a neat blue-and-yellow kitchen.

"I made coffee," he said.

"It smells good." Steve smiled. "Henry, this is Karen Barnett, from Los Angeles."

The old man shook my hand. I instantly was drawn to the sincerity in his eyes and his smile. Wearing jeans and a plain white shirt, he was tall and slim, well built for a man in his seventies.

Our host poured coffee into heavy blue mugs and we sat around the kitchen table. On the counter was a bread box almost exactly like the one my mother had owned. There were yellow dotted-swiss curtains at the window and a jelly jar with freshly picked flowers on the sill. On the wall was a ceramic plaque of a little girl holding a pie. A flowered tea towel hung on the oven handle.

Steve said, "You knew I'd bring Karen. What have you heard, Henry?"

The man glanced at me, then back at Steve. "I heard she was in town asking questions about the Saxons. Then I heard you knew her. Nobody seems to know how you knew her—there are different versions of that. I have to say I'm curious myself."

"We happened to meet the day she came into town. By pure chance. Did you know that somebody is threatening to harm her if she doesn't leave Tyrone?"

Paulson scowled. "I wish I could say that surprises me, but it doesn't."

"It surprises the hell out of me!"

The old man simply nodded.

Steve leaned across the table. "Henry, this whole town is so tight-lipped about the Saxons that our imaginations are starting to go wild. It took days just to dig out records to prove Wayne Saxon and his wife had ever lived—and ever died. Nobody's talking, and somebody feels threatened as hell by Karen's questions."

White eyebrows raised slightly. "I figured this was going to be the subject of our talk. What led you to me?"

"I was able to find out, with Erv Eckles's help, that you were with the police department at the time the Saxons died. I'm sure you know what we want—a description of the crime."

Henry Paulson looked from one of us to the other. I expected him to ask why, but he didn't, and the fact that he didn't made me very nervous. What did this man know?

His eyes squinted slightly. "You say you're from Los Angeles, Karen? Did you grow up there?"

"No, I come from Montana originally. My work is in California."

"Umm. Montana. I was there about ten years ago, drove across the whole state. Good air, nice country. What brought you to Tyrone then?"

I reached into my purse, pulled out the photo and handed it to him. "This. I was looking for this house. I've had...dreams about this house since I was young. I was shocked to find it in a photo among my mother's things. If you know what happened there, Mr. Paulson, you'd be doing me an enormous favor if you told me."

He was silent for a long time. "You know how they died. I know Erv found the coroner's report."

"Karen wants details," Steve said. "Who the witnesses were. She thinks she might have been there. We do know a boy was there."

The old man nodded casually, but his lips tightened. "This damned thing has haunted me for years, Steve. I never liked the way it was handled. I disapproved of the investigation. As God is my witness, I would have done it different. That's why, when you called me, I knew there was some good reason for asking now. Nobody ever came right out and brought it up all these years. But you're coming now. Maybe I been quiet but I haven't lied about it and I sure as hell won't lie to you. Dammit, of all people, not to you."

Steve's expression changed. He was sensing what I was—that Henry Paulson was about to do something that took courage.

"We got the call on a June morning," Henry began. "I remember it was June because that year early June was as wet and hot as mid-July and we had call after call from people stuck in mud and our only tow truck developed engine problems every time it went out. I was on the phone to Evensen trying to get another truck out here when the call came that there was a fire at the Saxon house and neighbors heard screaming from people possibly trapped inside. Me and Chuck Dyer and Bob Wentworth got there as fast as the fire department did. You remember Bob? Died what? Maybe six years ago. Chuck had just become sheriff then, maybe no more than a month before."

Henry Paulson was watching Steve closely. He paused as if watching Steve distracted him, bothered him. Abruptly he rose from the chair and went to the cabinet and took out a whiskey bottle.

"Want a drink, Steve? Karen?"

We both declined while he poured whiskey into a glass, took an enormous swallow and sat down again, bringing bottle and glass with him.

"This ain't easy, kids."

"Take your time," Steve said with forced patience. "We're interested in every detail you can recall. What did you find when you got to the Saxon house?"

"Two bodies. One was a woman near the stairway, and her husband's was in a room at the back of the house, off the kitchen, where the fire was."

My heart had already begun to pound. "The blue room with several windows looking out on the back yard?"

"Sounds right, yeah. We didn't have a chance to really look at the scene of Wayne Saxon's death because we had to get his body out before it was burned. Both were dead of gunshot wounds. You already know that, since you read the coroner's report. The gun was lying by the man's body with three unfired shells in it. We had to grab that, too—not even enough time to take any measurements. The woman had been shot once through the heart at close range, and the man had been shot in the head and also in the chest."

My mouth had gone bone dry. "In the dream I saw a lot of blood.

"That's accurate. The woman's wound bled profusely and she cut her head when she fell, and the head wound bled a lot, too. The front hall was bad. In fact that's how we knew a kid had been on the scene. His footprints were in the blood."

"Oh, God..." I said. "It really did happen...." I closed my eyes, but when I did, the vision rushed back. With a shaking hand, I poured a little whiskey from Henry's bottle into my coffee mug.

"Who was in the house?" Steve asked. "Whose footprints?"

"No one was in the house when we got there." He took a swallow of whiskey. "Your family lived next door at the time, Steve. Do you remember that you lived next door to the Saxons?"

"A few vague memories, not many."

"You and your cousin had a tree house in that big cottonwood tree. It's still there." Another swallow of whiskey. "You were eight, I think, when this tragedy happened. And you were at the Saxons' house that morning. The footprints in the blood were yours."

Chapter Twelve

Steve wheezed, *"Mine?"*

"You don't remember any of it, do you?"

"No! Henry, are you sure about this?"

"I wish I wasn't, Steve. The lab confirmed it. Footprints are easy to identify. I don't welcome the task of telling you, but on the other hand, I never thought it was fair for everybody to lie to you. They lied to you since you were a kid."

"Lied to me about what? About my being there? I don't get it, Henry! What the hell *is* all this? Why—"

Paulson interrupted. "This is rough stuff to have to hear. And it gets rougher, but if it's the truth you want . . ." He pushed the whiskey bottle in Steve's direction. "Here, have a swig. You need fortification." When Steve hesitated, Henry poured it for him and asked, "How much truth do you want?"

"All of it!"

"You don't know what you're asking."

"The sheriff and whoever else are hiding something. They're not in power here anymore, Henry. I am. If you're worried about repercussions, you have my protection, and you know that's not an idle promise."

"That ain't it. It's that once you hear this, nothing will be the same for you again. This ain't no little matter."

"We've guessed as much. Let's have it. You say the footprints were mine. Is that certain?"

"We knew they were yours from the size of them and the fact you never wore shoes in the summer. Later that day your mother found a bloodstained shirt in your room. The blood later proved to be Wayne Saxon's."

Steve tilted back on his chair. "Then I was the one who found the bodies?"

"More complicated than that. The murder weapon wasn't Saxon's. It had belonged to your father and it had your fingerprints on it."

Steve went pale. "I picked up the gun?"

"There was speculation that you might have fired it."

"*What?*"

"It was never proved. We do know, however, that you set the fire."

Staring at him, mouth agape, Steve said, "Henry, I was only eight years old!"

"Yep. Just turned. Chuck Dyer—who in my opinion is the biggest fool in Tyrone—took all that circumstantial evidence along with what else he knew about you and reconstructed the crime implicating you—a little kid, for God's sake!"

My hands had gone ice-cold. Steve sat as still as a statue. Henry's consumption of the whiskey was increasing rapidly.

"Reconstructed the crime..." Steve repeated in a hollow voice. "Okay, let's hear the reconstruction."

Henry's face was a ball of misery. He looked at his glass as he spoke. "Chuck Dyer, the ass, figured you were in the house and saw Wayne Saxon kill his wife. That part I go along with. The rest I don't. But Chuck was con-

vinced, still is, that when you saw the murder you became hysterical and enraged. Some of his reasoning you
wouldn't understand now, Steve. You were one tough
little kid. I never saw a kid as tough as you. You'd take
on anybody. Anyway, your footprints indicated you followed Saxon to the back room. He probably didn't know
you were there. Dyer thinks Saxon set down the gun and
you picked it up and shot him in the chest and then in the
head after he fell. You set the fire to cover the evidence,
then ran upstairs and out through a window over a
branch to your tree house. We do know you got out of
the house that way because you left a trail of blood.
There was kerosene and blood on your clothes.''

Steve retreated into a strange private silence.

Paulson met his eyes. ''So now you know, kid. Instead of trying to clear you, they covered it. Which means
they believed you were guilty.''

I heard my own voice squeak, ''An eight-year-old
committing murder? That's completely mad!''

''Mad as loons, all of them. I always said so.''

''I can't take this in,'' Steve said softly. ''It's just too
damned farfetched.''

''There were factors,'' Henry said, ''that indicated
murder. I don't know what the coroner's report said, or
if he was paid off at the time, but from the position of the
body and the gun, Wayne Saxon was probably killed by
somebody else.''

He looked hard at Steve. ''Your reputation didn't help.
You were a real hard kid to manage even at that age. You
had no dad and you ran with your cousin and his friends,
kids older than yourself, and that Glen was always a hel-
lion. Once, when you were six, you were caught firing
your dad's gun at tins cans. You were always in fights.
You even got kicked out of your Sunday-school class for

fighting. Your momma and your grandma had the devil's time with you." Henry smiled as if he'd just paid Steve a compliment. "The kind of kid you were, if you'd have witnessed a murder, people figured you had it in you to go gunnin' for the bad guy."

"That's ridiculous!" I blurted.

"Ridiculous as hair growing on a worm. Steve was smarter than that and he'd learned morals from his momma. Nevertheless, my boy, if you'd been an adult you'd have been indicted for murder. No other suspect. Me, I got my own theory. I think Wayne Saxon did shoot himself. I think Saxon was dead when you came into that room. He'd shot himself in the chest first and then in the head and the gun slid when he fell. You saw the body and the gun and, probably hysterical by then, picked up the gun and threw it back down."

"And set the fire..." Steve's voice was barely audible.

"The kerosene can was probably right there. Anyway, you knew the trouble was serious because you ran away and disappeared. It was three days before you were found—down by the river. Of course Dyer and Wentworth took your disappearance as guilt."

Steve began to choke. He grabbed for the whiskey. Henry watched him closely.

"So that's it," Steve muttered. "I was whisked out of town and my grandmother saw to it that none of this information ever got to the public, and the cover-up has been going on ever since."

"Your grandmother had Chuck Dyer in her pocket. Still does. Hell, she's got everybody in her pocket. But in this case, she was right to protect you. You were a tough kid, but you didn't kill anybody. I knew that, and your grandma and your momma knew it, too."

"How can you be so sure?" he asked softly.

Henry pounded the table. "You were barely eight years old!"

Steve rose and began to pace. "It's impossible for an eight-year-old kid to witness murder and not remember!"

"To the contrary. The opposite is true. I had some major concern about you. So much so that I drove over there to Evensen a few months later to see you. Even then the experience was blank in your mind. You didn't even remember who I was, and you and me had been friends. I took you fishing with me once."

"You'd have been severely traumatized," I said.

Henry nodded in agreement. "That was the word the doctor used. You momma took you to a doctor. I talked to him. They worked to deal with your trauma and convince you that any lingering 'bad feeling' you might've had was the aftereffects of a nightmare. You were young, impressionable, inclined to believe them when they reinvented your past."

Steve went to Henry's sink, filled a glass at the tap, and swallowed down the entire contents in one gulp. I watched, feeling his anguish as if we were one soul. He turned around. "Henry, that's a hell of a story! Tell me you're a senile old man subject to delusions."

"I wish to God I could tell you that, kid."

"Great. There are several people in this town who believe I'm a murderer." He swore and then apologized for his language. His voice was shaking.

"You didn't do it," the old man said.

"Yeah? If I was the angry kid you describe and I saw a man commit murder, maybe I did start firing that gun I liked to play with. How did Saxon get my father's gun?"

"Nobody knows that."

Steve wiped perspiration from his forehead. He had gone pale. "Couldn't there have been someone else involved?"

"There could've. Because of your grandma's clout in this town, nothing was ever investigated. It served your interest best to call it a suicide and drop the matter as fast as possible."

"So the inquiries just stopped?"

"Right. Like I said, evidence was tampered with, anyway, when we had to move the body and the weapon away from the flames. Only a handful of the people knew you were involved, and them that did were sworn to secrecy."

"Including you."

"I was as anxious to protect you as anybody, but I wanted to do it by finding more facts. I had no say in nothing. Dyer did what your grandma said. She'd been mainly responsible for him getting his job and he wouldn't go against her. So he dropped the matter and that was the end of it."

Steve's mouth was a grim line. He looked ill and his voice sounded strange. "Daphne must have believed I was guilty!"

"Nah. But she knew that if the town found out you were in the middle of that mess, the gossip wouldn't let up for the next hundred years."

"If Steve had asked you before, would you have told him?" I had to ask.

"Not when he was a little kid. But when a man asks for the truth, he gets it from me. We had no right to hide it. Anyway, Steve was right on the verge of finding out."

Steve sat down again, perspiration gleaming on his face and neck. "What do you mean, on the verge?"

"Karen showing up here. I figured that'd do it."

Steve and I stared at each other while our world crashed around us. All the time Henry Paulson had been talking he had been describing events I knew. Somewhere in the whirl I'd lost the place where the dream ceased and the fuzzy memories began. While Henry had been talking, I had been seeing, and feeling, all of it.

I asked, "Do you know me, Henry?"

"Doesn't take much intelligence to put together that you were the kid with Steve when he was found at the river."

"What do you mean?"

He looked at me as though I were as dense as night. "Right off, I realized you didn't know too much or you'd have told Steve. I mean, a tot of four or five suffering the trauma of seeing her momma killed..."

I burst into tears and stumbled to my feet. "What are you saying?"

Steve stood up then, too, and engulfed me in his arms. He held me tight against his chest. Henry Paulson made gurgling apologies.

"Don't apologize," Steve said. "We had suspicions but we just couldn't get any facts."

Sniffing, I forced myself away from the protective comfort of Steve's warmth. "My mother? You're sure?"

But my parents were Maureen and John Barnett! I screamed inside myself while I tried desperately to recall any memory, any at all, from my early years. There was none, only the photos. If what Henry said was true, then Maureen and John Barnett knew me when I was a Saxon. It was possible. They could have been friends, or even relatives of Mary's and Wayne's.

"The Saxon children...?" I began.

"They were shipped out of town as fast as Steve was. Faster. None of us ever knew where to. We figured relatives took the kids. There were a couple of people at the funeral, but from out of town."

I felt dizzy, almost faint.

Steve said, "Karen, you don't look very good."

"I don't feel very good. I'd better leave. Henry, we're so deeply indebted to you..."

He frowned. "Kids, if I was in your shoes, I'd want the truth, too. You deserve to know." Henry shook Steve's hand and squeezed mine gently. His eyes were sad.

"This town ain't been good to you," he said to Steve at the door.

"What you've told me today explains a lot."

"I thought it might." He opened his garage door as soon as we were in the car.

The street was deserted. No one saw us leave the Paulson house. We rode in dark silence, each caught in painful thoughts of our own, thoughts strangling around agony, disbelief, confusion and anger.

Skipper's exuberant greeting was like a splash of cold water to fevered heads. Two zombies, we settled onto the couch in Steve's den.

I was the one who broke the silence. "Steve, what have I unleashed by stirring up the past? I'm so sorry."

"Why, Karen? Do you think it would be better if I'd never known?"

"Maybe. Maybe they were right to protect you."

"Hell no, they weren't right. And what about you? Your parents never told you..."

"Never told me who I am?"

"We can see why Daphne desperately wanted you out of town. You're like a ghost returning—the kid whose father I might have killed—"

I put my fingers to his lips. "Don't say that! Don't!"

"There's been enough hiding from the truth, Karen. Let's not you and I do it."

I sighed shakily. "*Could* I have been with you at the river? Could we have run away and hidden?"

"The other day when you drank water from my hands, we were remembering...another time. Déjà vu. Yes, you were with me at the river."

"Steve, my identity has risen out of me, up and out, leaving me absolutely empty. How can I be their daughter? Why would my parents never have told me?"

"Isn't it obvious? For the same reason I was never told. What could they have said? That your father killed your mother and himself? They couldn't talk to a kid about that kind of a past."

I sat back and closed my eyes. "Whoever I am, I must have a brother somewhere, and you and I . . . you and I were children together. . . ."

"Until that day. I don't think either of us were ever children again, after that day."

"We were both in the house. It wasn't a dream at all."

"Henry said I set the fire. Why would I do that?"

"Who knows what a kid that scared would do?"

"Something doesn't quite add up. Henry admitted the suicide was not absolutely substantiated, that Saxon might have been murdered, and you think there was someone else in the house. Someone else might have killed him."

"After the hypnosis, I'm sure someone else was there."

"You said the house was full of kids."

"Yes . . ."

"Your brother."

"Or . . . or your cousin."

"Glen? Why do you think it could have been Glen?"

"I don't know. I thought about Glen when Henry Paulson was talking. When he mentioned the river, I thought about Glen."

"Good Lord, Karen, so did I!" He paused thoughtfully. "Glen told me once that, when we were kids, we used to hide things down by the river. I don't remember it, but he showed me the places and evidence of our hiding spots. People still talk about how Glen used to get in trouble for stealing. He was a little delinquent, and his dad always got him off."

"McGil mentioned it."

He nodded. "Between the two of us, we must have been a handful. Daphne always violently disapproved of my friendship with Glen. She's never liked him or his father. Calls them black sheep, and never passes up the chance to mention Glen's flawed reputation."

"But not yours?"

"No, never mine. As far as Daphne is concerned I'm an angel."

"But you've been into trouble yourself, haven't you? Your cousin told me today that you're an ex-convict."

Cold fury filled his eyes. "Glen told you that?"

I felt his hurt and anger, and softened my voice. "Is it true?"

"Yes. But I'm damned surprised he told you."

"Why? Because it's another of Tyrone's secrets?"

"That's right." He rubbed his chin. "Cuz and I had better have a little talk."

I winced. "It's incredible the way this town protects you! From the past you don't remember, and from the past you do remember...."

"They're not protecting me. They're protecting themselves."

"But from what? From you?"

I didn't like Steve's laugh. It was sinister. "From their own guilt. They convicted me of a crime I didn't commit. I served three years in prison before the guilty person confessed."

"Steve! What do you mean?"

He shifted his body, not wanting to talk about it, I knew. "When I was in college, I worked here in summers at the hardware store where I'd worked all during high school. When the store was robbed and police said it was an inside job, they indicted me. My reputation as a troublemaker didn't help. I was sentenced to five years and served three before the store owner's son confessed—after he'd had some religious experience. I realize now that Dyer believed I was a criminal since the age of eight."

"Three years of your life in prison? That's horrible!"

"I finished law school in prison. Some alma mater, huh? Even though I was acquitted, the whole episode jeopardized my chances of having a successful attorney's career. The leaders of Tyrone were so guilt ridden—with Daphne leaning really hard on them—that they offered me a position I was more or less forced to take. They wanted a strong leader in the mayor's office and I wanted a job. Part of the deal was keeping their mouths shut about my time in prison. Glen broke that promise today."

His eyes flashed anger. "I didn't plan to stay long in Tyrone, but after I took office as mayor I found I liked the job. Glen and a few others had begun planning a resort development around the river. I've been able to block that effort. As long as I'm in office I'll keep on blocking it, while Glen keeps enticing guys like McGil with promises of big profits from commercializing. He won't give up and neither will I."

"You and Glen butt heads a lot, don't you?"

"Always have. My cousin resents the way I run this town. He wanted the mayor's job but he didn't have a chance against me, not with my backing. I ran for mayor deliberately to keep him out, and to save my river."

"You have power, and you wield it like a pro."

"What good is power if you don't use it?"

"Why would Glen betray your past to me? Could it have been to try to scare me out of town?"

"Nah. It's jealousy. I don't think Glen has anything to do with the threats against you. Daphne is doing that."

"I wonder."

"Glen couldn't know who you are, Karen."

"He could if Daphne told him, or the sheriff."

"If he knew your identity he'd have told me. Glen and I have had our serious differences, but under it all, there's a loyalty."

I smiled. "I'll bet he led you down the garden path when you were kids."

"And got me in trouble constantly. He admits it. That's probably how I got so tough—learning to stand up to my brat of a big cousin."

I looked out at the night sky through the plate-glass window of his den, piecing together the several tragedies of Steve's life. "Was she a local girl—the girl you were engaged to?"

"No. I met her at the university. When I was back here working in the summer she was in Europe with her mother."

"Let me venture a guess. After you were arrested, she didn't want to be engaged to a criminal."

"Exactly."

"Even if you were innocent?"

"I was convicted. That was proof enough for her family—and for her. Hell, I can't blame her. She cared what people thought. Even if she'd believed me, which she didn't, she'd have left."

"No wonder you're bitter."

"Let's just say I learned the hard way not to trust people."

"Not to trust women, you mean."

"What can I say? That's what love gets you."

"You're convinced all women are like her."

"All *people* are like her. When a woman you love betrays you, though, it's hard to swallow."

A long silence ensued before I said, "You've been betrayed often. No wonder you can't trust others."

"It's how the world is." He wanted to leave the subject.

"Your world, maybe. Not mine."

Steve mussed my hair playfully. "You're a romantic, aren't you? Yep, a romantic. And I'm a realist. Shall we fix some dinner?"

"I can't eat."

"Then why not just lean against me and try to relax. You've been through hell today."

"So have you." His chest was hard and solid against me. Maybe he was the only solid thing in the world. His strength was the only thing I was sure of, the only thing I could rely on. Had that been so before in our lives?

I asked, "Steve, did a little boy once protect a little girl from an experience too horrible for her to face? Were we really there together? Was that why I felt instant comfort and trust when we met?"

He smiled softly. "And is it why I felt I knew you?"

"It is, isn't it? That terrible thing neither of us can remember—we lived it together, and you protected me even then."

I closed my eyes and welcomed the feel of his body against mine and wished he could care as much for me as I cared for him. But he never would. He was too determined never to care deeply about any woman. He liked me, and that was going to have to be enough.

He rubbed my temples gently. "First thing tomorrow we're going to confront my grandmother about all this. It's high time Daphne put an end to her pretending."

Steve was subdued, almost sullen, the rest of the night and the next morning. I knew he was more upset about Henry's revelations than he wanted to let on. I sensed his inner turmoil as much as he sensed mine.

DAPHNE KNEW something was wrong the moment she saw Steve's face. She glanced at me with a strange expression before she smiled and led us into her elegant sitting room.

"Goodness, Steve, dear. From the looks of you, something is the matter."

"Several things." He waited until she was settled comfortably into her favorite armchair. "First of all, the Citizens Auxiliary is threatening Karen with voodoo dolls."

Her eyes got wide. "Voodoo?"

"Who plays with voodoo dolls?"

"You know perfectly well I have collected voodoo dolls."

"Yes. It took me a while before I remembered."

"Many people know about my interest in such things. Someone is trying to make it look like I support this . . . this terrorist group! How dare they! This is a matter for the police. Have you informed the police?''

"Do you really want me to?"

"Where is this doll? I'd like to see it."

"Steve destroyed it," I said.

"Destroyed the evidence?"

His impatience hardened his voice. "Dammit, don't lie to me, Daphne. For once don't lie to me. I know you made that stupid doll because you wanted to put a stop to Karen's questions."

"Steve, what is the matter with you?"

He sat down. The lighting in the room was dim; the curtains were parted only slightly. Daphne Hayes wore a white lace-trimmed blouse and dark skirt similar to the clothes she'd worn the first time we met. Diamond-and-pearl earrings sparkled when she turned her head. Steve, in his jeans and short-sleeved summer shirt looked out of place in the classic elegance of this room.

He answered, "What's wrong with me is that I heard a disturbing story last night about the morning Wayne and Mary Saxon died. Why was I never told that I was implicated in Wayne Saxon's death?"

One could only describe the look in the woman's eyes as hate when she glanced at me. Steve caught the glance and said quickly, "No, Karen didn't tell me. She had no idea who she was until last night."

Shaken, the old woman asked, "Who told you such a ridiculous thing?"

"Someone who felt it was my right to know."

"Steve, my dear, you must try to understand the circumstances. You were a victim, an innocent victim. You suffered enough over that dreadful experience and deserved to have it put behind you forever. Oh, those horrid people!"

"I'm not a child now. I should have been told."

She fingered the pearls at her throat. "There were times I wanted to talk to you about it, but it was just too painful and I could never bring myself to do it. That fool of a sheriff, trying to implicate an innocent child. I'm glad you finally fired him."

"Is there any proof I was innocent? If there is, I'd rather not live with the question."

"Well not...proof. Common sense is proof enough."

"What do *you* think happened? Wayne committed suicide?"

"Of course. There is no other explanation." She turned to me. "Karen, do you see all the pain your questioning has caused?"

I met her cold gaze. "When I started asking questions, I had no idea Steve was involved with that house in any way."

"The investigation was stopped," Steve said. "How did you manage that?"

She was shocked. "What was there to investigate? You did pick up the gun, we know that. No doubt you were frantic and frightened. It hardly constitutes a case for murder!"

"It was my father's gun."

"Wayne Saxon got hold of it somehow. Your father probably gave it to him. They were neighbors. Steve, don't look at me like that. I'd have done anything to protect you from those incompetent hysterical police."

"And you still would."

"Of course!"

The housekeeper appeared in the doorway carrying a silver tray with one of the most ornate and beautiful tea services I had ever seen.

"Thank you, Mildred," Daphne said. "I hope you included some of those lovely little mint bakery cookies."

"Yes, and some cinnamon tarts."

"How fine, perfect."

She was so cool, so completely in control. Unflappable, Steve sat scowling, irritated that his grandmother made so light of the lies she'd raised him on.

Obviously Daphne felt that her motives were justified, and it was hard for me not to agree. As a woman, I could understand the lengths another woman would go to to protect a child she loved. Steve was all she had, and it was true, he was a victim. I couldn't share Steve's anger at her.

As soon as the housekeeper left the room, Daphne proceeded with the ritual of serving the tea. With a silver server, she placed cookies slowly and carefully on each of three china plates.

He said, "An incorrigible child who played with real guns might actually have pulled the trigger."

Her hand began to shake. "Of course not! Are you mad?"

"Did anyone actually see what happened?"

"How could anyone..." Daphne glanced involuntarily at me—a very slight eye movement, but I caught it. *She believes I was a witness,* I thought with panic. *She's known who I am from the first day I came. She'd lied about the Saxon girl's age, purposely adding on five years to throw us off the scent. She knows I was there. She knows Steve and I ran away and were found together. Who more than Daphne could have wanted me out of here before Steve found out what he now had?* Her worst fears had happened. Because of me. Steve now knew he was a murder suspect and he'd never been cleared. She *had* tried voodoo to scare me away, hadn't she?

Trembling slightly, Daphne lifted the silver teapot and proceeded to pour. "Sugar?" she asked me.

"One cube."

I rose to take the cup and saucer from her. When Steve's grandmother reached out to hand me the tea, I went suddenly ice-cold—almost to the point of fainting.

Her diamond-and-ruby ring caught the light. The ring was the one I'd seen in my nightmare! It was the same ring I had seen lifted from a hand that lay in a pool of blood!

Chapter Thirteen

There was no mistaking the ring! I'd seen it a hundred times in the colored shadows of my dream. Numbly I accepted the teacup and saucer and managed not to spill the tea. My mind was whirring so fast I couldn't shake off the dizziness.

How could Daphne have that ring?

I could barely fight down the impulse to ask, but a strong warning sounded within me. What would I say? *I saw that same ring in my dream...saw it stolen from the hand of Mary Saxon?* I would not have been able to control my voice. I could not deal with thinking of that hand as that of my mother. Not enough time had elapsed, and not enough solid evidence, for me to make that complete shift of identity.

Steve was staring at me. "Karen, is something the matter?"

I stammered foolishly. "It's all so...horrible...."

"Yes, it is," his grandmother agreed, sipping her tea. "Surely you can understand why I could never discuss it with you, Steve. I never wanted this unfortunate tragedy to have to be part of your life."

"Things won't go away by pretending they never happened."

"They can, if no one comes along to dredge them up."

"Don't blame Karen for this."

"Whom shall I blame then?"

His eyes flashed. "If you have to put blame, then blame yourself for not being honest with me. Blame Chuck Dyer for being too spineless to go against your wishes. Blame this whole damned town. If they hadn't believed I might be guilty, they wouldn't have felt the need to hide the truth."

"That isn't so! We were protecting a child from the memories of a very painful experience."

"A child? I asked you about the Saxons two days ago."

Steve frightened me when he was angry. I wondered if he, too, noticed that Daphne didn't ask any questions about my identity. Of course, she knew.

Steve said. "Afterward I ran away. I was found on a river island with the Saxons' daughter."

His grandmother sipped her tea. "Yes."

"Do you recall her name?"

She straightened. "They had a daughter named Christina."

Christina? At the sound of the name, a shiver shot through me, a sudden awful fear so devastating I wanted to run screaming from the room. Run in search of something, I didn't know what. Christina was my name, not Karen....

My head spun. Steve was suddenly at my side. "Karen, you look sick. Do you need to lie down?"

"I just want to go...outside...."

He helped me to my feet, supporting me with his strength. "We have to go, Daphne."

She said, "Oh, Karen, dear, can I help you?"

I shook my head against Steve's shoulder.

On legs of rubber, clinging to Steve, I somehow got down the steps of the front porch.

"You're ill," he said.

"I felt so...desperate. The sound of that name...Christina...sent such a cold cloak of loneliness over me...I can't get warm. I'm sorry...I must seem—"

"Don't be sorry! I don't know what's holding either one of us together any longer. The name is familiar?"

"Yes. So is the ring..." I murmured.

"What?"

His grandmother's huge house loomed behind us like a mean hungry monster. All I wanted to do was get out of its shadow and back into sunshine.

"Maybe I'd better carry you."

"In this neighborhood? It'd make the evening news."

Steve's house was only a couple of blocks away; I could make it that far. But in between was the Saxon house, the house whose secrets belonged to us....

By the time we reached the Saxon house, I was feeling stronger, but emotionally I thought I'd never feel normal again. We walked up the shady path and sat down on the front steps.

"Does it frighten you to be here?" he asked.

"Not as much as before. Isn't that odd?"

"Maybe knowing what happened, however bad, is still preferable to the unknown."

"Steve, there was another witness to both deaths, I'm sure. Whoever that person was, he doesn't want either of us remembering. He would want me out of town, not to protect you but to protect himself."

"I've been thinking the same thing. It could mean you're in real danger. Someone who killed once could kill again, especially if he believes you're about to expose him.''

"But Daphne all but admitted the voodoo was her doing, to keep me away from you. She'd lied too about my age."

He sighed. "I know. She thought she was protecting me." He studied me. "Aside from that I think there was someone else there, and so do you."

I shuddered. "Murder with what motive?"

"Who knows? They said Mary was much younger than her husband, and another man might have been in the picture. I can't believe the murder was preplanned, though, or it wouldn't have happened in broad daylight with a house full of kids."

"A robbery would have been preplanned."

"Henry didn't mention anything about a robbery."

"Henry didn't know about the ring."

"Oh yeah, the diamond ring you talked about."

Above us in the trees birds were singing and in the grass insects buzzed and chirped. Somewhere down the street an electric lawn mower droned. Sounds of summer. Skipper found us sitting there on the porch of the empty house. He greeted us with a quick lick and then went about his business of sniffing out the dark area under the stairs where a cat or a squirrel might have been hiding.

I took his hand. "Steve, I just saw that ring again. Your grandmother is wearing it."

His jaw dropped; his boot heels scraped against the wooden step. "You must be mistaken, Karen. You couldn't recognize—"

"Oh, yes, I can recognize it! I saw the ring vividly in the dream, and I assure you it's the same one."

"Why didn't you ask her about it? It's important to know who she got it from! Don't you see? Whoever had the ring before Daphne might be the person we're trying to identify."

"When I saw the ring in real life I went into mild shock and my brain shut down. And then she hit me with that name—Christina—and I felt faint."

"You are Christina. You must be."

"I must be. It feels right, but then it doesn't. Oh, Steve, if I am, she has to know it!"

I turned around and looked up at the massive haunted house behind us—once such a beautiful home, now surrounded only by sadness. Who'd have thought one could feel sorry for a house? But I did. The horrible tragedy followed by years of abandonment were so unfair.

"I want to go inside again," I said. "Alone this time, just to wander around in the shadows and try to remember who I am."

"I understand. You could go in now but I don't have the key with me."

I stood up and wiped dust from the back of my skirt. As we stepped down from the porch, I noticed a curtain fall in the window next door. Someone was watching us. Steve had seen the movement, too.

"The lady who sees ghosts?" I asked.

"The same. Stella's been spreading her ghost story around the neighborhood. There are two people on the side porch across the street who have been staring at us ever since we got here."

"Great. Just what you need. Another scandal. Now you're keeping company with the ghost."

"Scandal is the heartbeat of Tyrone."

Skipper led the way home. When we entered Steve's house the telephone was ringing.

Steve picked it up and scowled at the first of the message. "Oh, yeah. I hear you've been blazing a wide trail with your mouth."

It had to be Glen. Not wanting to hear an argument, I went into the guest room, where both of us had slept again last night, and changed from my summer dress into jeans and a loose comfortable shirt. When I returned to the kitchen, Steve was still on the phone.

"I'm not in the mood to discuss it," he said, holding the receiver with his shoulder while he peeled a banana. "Okay, okay, I'll meet you. My office. Fine. I'll be right there."

He hung up, shaking his head. "Want a banana?"

"No thanks. Are you going to tell Glen what you learned about the Saxons?"

"It would be the same as putting an ad in the paper to tell Glen. He's acting funny. I think he's up to no good. By the way, he says he's sorry he shot off his mouth about me."

"While you're in town, I'd like to go back to the Saxon house."

"Are you sure? The ghost was in there last night."

"Hmm. I'm the ghost, remember?"

"Maybe you are. Maybe you go there at night in your dreams. Astral project out of your body and become a spirit."

"Don't laugh. I've actually wondered if that's possible."

"So have I." He took a key from the kitchen desk and handed it to me. "But we agreed nothing psychic's going on. I hate to let you out of my sight. Maybe you'd better come with me."

"The Saxon house is the safest place in town. Nobody else will go in there. Nobody else can even get in. Please don't baby me. I'll be fine in there."

"All right. I'll drop you off there, and we'll put your car in my garage so no one will know you're in the neighborhood. If you're not here when I get back, I'll go over there. Okay?"

"Sure. What does Glen want?"

"Who knows? He has a talent for making a big deal out of nothing. He's been talking to McGil again."

"Maybe he's learned something more."

"Maybe he has. With Cuz Glen I never know."

I DIDN'T SEE a sign of any neighbor from the front porch of the Saxon house as I was unlocking the door, but that didn't mean someone wasn't watching from behind dark windows. The two locks gave easily. I opened the door and waved Steve on. When he drove away, I was left alone with my confused and conflicting emotions on the doorstep of the house of my nightmares, where the ghost had walked in last night's moonlight.

To enter this house was the same as entering my dream. Yet I had to absorb everything I'd learned and to understand what I might never understand. The long-abandoned house was as still as death. The second I closed the door behind me and locked it so that I couldn't be followed, I began to feel a sensation so eerie it scared me. It wasn't anything I'd ever felt in the dream, nor anything I'd ever felt in life. The name Christina went on and off in my head like a flashing neon light. Was it my name? What was this sudden devastating loneliness? Could it be my failure to connect with my own identity?

Perhaps. I had as strong an identity as Karen Barnett. But I had been here twenty-five years ago in this house! Who was I then?

My sneakers made no sound as I walked through the house. I kept seeing the ring on Daphne's finger. I didn't recall describing to Steve exactly what I had witnessed— the ring removed from the hand of Mary Saxon. I wished now I had told him so that he would understand what had upset me so.

It didn't make sense that her husband would take it. Nor did it make sense that someone else would run up to the dead woman immediately after her husband shot her and strip a diamond ring from her finger. What *had* happened?

Daphne Hayes, in seeming innocence, was wearing that ring twenty-five years later. Why hadn't I just asked her where she got it from? If I had, we might know by now who else had been there that day.

Through the house's silence I heard the screams again. I stood on the landing of the stairs, on the spot where a woman who must have been my mother had died, and I heard terrible screams. Again. It was hardly bearable to stand there, but I forced myself to do so, and to see again, and to listen . . .

There was no sound. And yet . . . something was here! I could feel another presence in the house. My heart began to flutter. What had that woman next door—Stella— really seen at the high window at night?

The ghost? Was it here? Desperately I tried to shake off the feeling that I wasn't alone, but it was no use. There *was* something here—or someone—somewhere in the house. Listening, I could hear nothing now but the shrieks of silence.

I looked up the dimly lighted staircase. As before, it was the third floor of the house that lured me. The last time, with Steve, shrill muffled voices had filled my head. This time the voices were gone. In their place was the whispery sound of wind blowing through a broken window high above me. Wind like someone breathing—up there.

I forced one foot in front of the other, climbing at a sloth's pace. My palms were cold and sweating by the time I reached the second-floor landing. Since I hadn't explored this floor, I decided to do so now. I turned down the shadowy hallway, peering in through the open door of each bedroom. The wallpaper in these rooms was faded but well preserved, and the wood floors were beautiful under the layer of dust. The largest room contained a fireplace. The bedrooms and bathrooms with their lovely fixtures looked as if they'd been abandoned only months ago instead of years ago.

I was standing by the fireplace of the large bedroom when I heard a small shuffling sound from the floor above me. This time, it was not my imagination; something or someone was in the house! I tried to fight my panic, remembering Steve had said squirrels could get into broken upper windows. I might even have heard the branches of the giant cottonwood scraping against the windows. Except that there was almost no wind.

The noise came again, different from before, this time a creaking sound like footsteps! There definitely was something on the floor above. I was in the far north wing; the blue-and-yellow dormer room would be directly over me. It was from that room that the sounds emanated. I felt an irresistible tug toward them.

I scolded myself for my fears. I didn't believe in ghosts, and what if I did? Ghosts didn't attack people; they just sort of floated about, didn't they? Ghosts were only spirits, after all. Even if there was a ghost in here, how could it hurt me?

Slowly I made my way back along the second-floor hallway to the foot of the stairs, where I stood looking up. I could hear the pounding of my own heart. The small horizontal window at the top of the stairs, filthy as it was, filtered in mellow white sunlight from outside, lighting the upper hall and third-floor landing.

My head went light. My breaths became shallow because I was afraid to breathe. My hands were cold and sweating, but I just kept climbing up the stairway of my childhood terror.

I was in the center of the upstairs hallway when a muffled moan floated out into the silence. I froze. The moan had come from the room at the far end of the corridor—the blue-and-yellow dormer room, the room where the ghost had been seen.

Through my trembling, I was struck by a powerful realization: by now I associated that room with myself to the point where I felt I myself was in there, even now— my identity, my child self. My child self! That was what my search was about, my emptiness. . . .

Approaching the room, I could taste blood from biting my lip. I hadn't imagined the moan; it wasn't ghostly, it was human. From the open doorway, I scanned as much of the room as I could see. First I saw the green leafy branches of the cottonwood tree outside the window. Then the dusty white window seat.

Cautiously I stepped inside, knowing, somehow sensing, that I would not leave this room the same person I was when I walked in.

Back in the shadows of the far corner of the room crouched the small willowy figure of a woman.

Chapter Fourteen

A woman—not a ghost! Surely a ghost wouldn't sit hunched in a corner, knees up, head buried in her arms as if she was crying!

The figure didn't move, but a moan moved from her throat. I thought, *she's real!* The dark form, silhouetted against the sunshine streaming through the window, clad in jeans and a blue T-shirt, was a living woman, not a ghost! She had not heard me enter.

Not wishing to startle her, I tried to speak, but no voice came. When I cleared my throat softly, she raised her head from her folded arms.

She stared at me in disbelief. Frozen to the floor, I stared back. Her face was mine! The eyes of the ghost were my own eyes! She was the mirror image of me! The ghost was me! This couldn't be happening. I was dreaming again.

I stood in numbed silence. The ghost of me stared back. I have no idea how long we stared at each other, but somewhere in the vortex of that agonized time, she spoke.

"Karen?"

I opened my mouth; still I had no voice. She knew my name!

"Karen?" Her shoulders straightened.

"Who...?" I managed in a raspy whisper. "Who are you?"

"I'm Christina."

"I don't understand!"

She didn't smile; her eyes were strangely blank. "I'm Christina. I've come home."

Who was she? Was she me? Was she the child in me come home? My brain whirled. No, she was not a child, she was a woman like me....

Tears sprang to my eyes. I rushed forward with an uncontrollable urge to physically connect with her, to assure myself she was flesh, not spirit. Kneeling, I touched her arm, and it was warm flesh.

"Christina?" My head was bursting with pain and confusion and the ache of almost grasping, almost remembering....

"Our things are gone," she said in a flat dull voice. "Scotty and Mister Pierre and Ella Font. All gone. Everybody is gone." She reached out and grabbed me and held me so tight it hurt. "Karen, everybody is gone!"

I closed my eyes and felt the tears slide down my cheeks.

"Mommy's gone...."

When I felt her heart beat against mine it all came rushing back. "Christina!" My cry echoed through the empty halls of the house. "Christina!"

Our clutch was so tight neither of us could breathe. "Oh, God...oh, God..." I uttered. "These years...how can it be that I forgot you...?"

"You didn't forget. You came home."

Memories flooded back. Sisters...twins...I had a twin sister. In misty dreams of my mind I had seen her sometimes in the distance and thought I was seeing myself!

Now, through the blur of painful joyful tears, even now, I sensed something horribly wrong. Her eyes...her voice...something wrong...

How did she get here? Where had she been?

"It's been so long!" I sobbed.

"Yes. The pond was frozen and now it's full of frogs again. We're not little anymore."

I took her hands in mine, felt the beat of her pulse. Even my breath found the rhythm of hers. Only when I looked into her eyes could I begin to comprehend what was happening. I didn't want to let her go, not ever. If I let her go, the present might rush back and I would have to find some way to explain it.

"It's been a long, long time," she whispered.

"This was our room, wasn't it?"

"Don't you remember Ella Font and the blue bear?"

I shook my head. "I don't remember."

"I do. You called me Chrissy then."

Spinning moments. I tried to grasp some meaning. In my investigations, no one had mentioned that the Saxons had twin daughters! Why not? And the boy? It was McGil who'd said the Saxons had a son—a wiry little kid in a cowboy hat. Was it his mistake? He'd only assumed the child was a boy? It was possible. Probable. Daphne had known; she had to know. Perhaps even Glen remembered. They didn't want me to learn I had a sister! What a cruel and sinister act.

I asked, "How did you get in here?"

"Key."

"Where did you get a key?"

"I stole it once and kept it in my secret box with the others. She never knew. She thought it got lost."

"Who never knew?"

"That old Mrs. Hayes."

I reeled. Daphne was in contact with Christina? How could she be? "When did you last see Mrs. Hayes?"

"When I was here before. Two years ago, maybe. I lost track of time."

"Where do you live, Christina . . . Chrissy?"

"In the willows."

"The willows?"

"Like wind in the willows. I live in the willows."

"Will you show me where you live?"

"I can't. I'm home now and so are you and here we'll stay. We'll stay! How come you don't know anything, Karen? I know where *you've* been."

"You do?"

"You've been at Aunt Maureen's and Uncle John's house. They said I couldn't go with you because I was sick and I had to go to the willows."

Aunt and Uncle? Maureen and John Barnett? They *had* adopted me! My mother must have been Mary Saxon's sister. Yes, that would explain the early photos. And Christina? My twin? Where had she been? And how could she just suddenly appear? Getting more desperate by the second, I was starting to wonder if she even knew how she got here. It was painfully evident that while my only reality was the present, my sister's only reality was the past.

In strained silence, we slid away from the present. Bits and pieces were starting to filter back. This room, toys, a picture of a clown on the wall. A meadowlark in the tree outside the window chorused a song of childhood that once I had often heard but then forgotten, until now.

"The bird is singing again," Christina said happily.

My heart went out to her. "Finding you," I said, "is finding the missing piece of myself. I've always felt something was missing."

"I knew you'd find me someday."

She was here the day our parents died! The day Steve and I ceased to be children, Christina got caught in her childhood forever.

I asked, "Do you remember Steve?"

"I don't like Steve. He likes you better. Steve loves you—everybody says so. You love him, too, even though Daddy says he's naughty. Daddy doesn't like him and neither do I."

"Steve is a man now." I was getting the feeling back in my body. "How long have you been here? Were you here all night?"

"I don't know how long."

Christina *had* been here at night. A large flashlight lay on the window seat. She was the ghost Stella Barrow had glimpsed in the upper window. And she had been here before—two years before—and maybe before then. She'd had a key for a long time.

Christina had come to reclaim her childhood and find me. She had walked these creaking black rooms in the night, her flashlight showing from the windows, giving rise to stories of a ghost.

She looked thin and fragile. Wiping at the tears that stained my cheeks, I asked, "What have you had to eat?"

"I brought cupcakes. Remember? Chocolate, your favorite."

"How long do you plan to stay here?"

"She always finds me. That old Mrs. Hayes. She finds me and takes the key, but I have a whole box of keys. A friend made them for me in a store."

Anger was overtaking me. Daphne was involved in the welfare of my twin sister? How could she keep such a thing from me? To protect her grandson, of course. But how had she come to be involved in Christina's life?

Unanswered questions—I was sick to death of them. I wanted only to curl up here with Christina in that soft splash of sunshine that warmed the wooden floor of this blue-and-white room where we'd been children together. I wanted to shut out cruel time, cruel reality, and pretend that there was no such thing as either.

But reality wouldn't evaporate, vanish. I had to try to think what to do. Wherever my sister lived, someone would be missing her, and probably knew where to come to find her. I didn't want to be separated from her again; we needed time. But we couldn't stay and wait to be discovered.

"Chrissy, we have to get out of here."

"No!"

"Before someone finds us. We have to go someplace safer."

"Oh. Where do we go then? If we go outside they'll see us."

"You're right." I thought for a minute. "I have a car a couple of blocks away. If I could drive it into this garage, we could get in without being seen, and you could simply duck out of sight in the car. Can we get the garage door open?"

"The door to the garage from the kitchen is nailed shut, but there's a little window from the mudroom."

I rose. "Let's go see."

"This is fun, Karen! I can get through that window."

She held my hand on the stairway. At the top landing her hesitation confirmed what I already knew: Christina, too, remembered. I wondered if I should quiz her about the past, but there was no time to try. We had to get out now before rumors of a "ghost" reached Daphne's ears and she acted fast. Together we crept down the stairs through the dining room to the kitchen.

She wriggled through the window easily and let herself down onto the floor of the large dark garage. I handed her the flashlight.

"Don't open the door yet, just see if it will open from inside."

I watched the light beam move through the dimly lighted area. In a moment she called back, "It's a hand latch. It'll open."

"Good. Just wait here, Christina. I'll be back in five minutes. I'll come in the front, in case people are watching, and then we'll open the garage door and I'll drive in so you can sneak into the car."

"This is fun," she repeated.

Actually I was back in four minutes, because I ran all the way to Steve's house and jumped in my car. I hadn't had time to really absorb what was happening, but right now what mattered more than anything else was getting Christina out of that house before she was discovered.

With my car parked close to the garage door, I rushed to the front door, locked the door behind me again and raced toward the kitchen. Christina was still in the garage, waiting by the little window.

She giggled as I struggled through the small opening. "You're thinner than I am!" I said.

My sister might have been confused about reality, but she knew exactly what was going on now as she climbed into the back seat of my car and crouched on the floor, muttering, "The neighbors can't see me!"

I unlatched the garage door, backed the car out, and then jumped out and closed the garage door again. The inside bar fell into place and locked itself.

"Where are we going?" came the muffled voice from behind.

I pulled into Steve's drive and on into his garage. "We're already there. You can come out."

He wasn't home yet, for which I was thankful. I led Christina into the kitchen. "I'm going to fix you a hot meal of whatever I can find in here."

She looked about curiously. "Whose house is this?"

"It's Steve's."

"No it isn't! I've been in his house!"

"It's his new house."

"I want to go home."

"Honey, you're safe with me. No one knows where we are. And Steve is our friend."

Calm as I sounded for her sake, I was on the edge of panic. We didn't have much time before we were discovered. So touched was I by her love and trust, I had to constantly fight back tears. "Do you like eggs?"

"Scrambled with catsup. You remember."

I smiled and nodded. Steve had eggs, bread and two apples. I peeled the apples and set them frying in butter. "Chrissy, are you happy where you live?"

"In the willows I talk about you and they think I'm making you up. They say there isn't a real Karen."

"We'll have to show them, won't we?"

"Yes!" This idea delighted her. It took every shred of strength I had to keep from crying out in pain. My heart was breaking.

I added cinnamon and sugar to the cooked apples, and served them with the scrambled eggs and toast. Christina had barely begun to eat when I heard Steve's car in the drive. The sound of his engine stopping set a new wave of panic through me.

"I hear a car," I said with forced calm. "I think it's Steve. You go ahead and eat and I'll go see if it's him."

"Okay," she agreed. "But I don't like Steve."

Steve was surprised to see me rush out onto the front porch. Thank God he was alone.

"Karen, what's the matter? You've been crying."

I pulled him quickly into the privacy of his living room. "Steve..." I began, my voice shaking.

He circled his arm around me and asked gently, "What's happened?"

"The Saxons had two daughters—twins. When I went back to the house... Christina was there."

"What are you talking about?"

"Shh, please whisper. She's in the kitchen. Christina is my twin sister, Steve. It's true! I don't know how she got back to the Saxon house, or where she's been. She isn't well. I think she must live in some kind of institution."

He stared unblinking until his blue eyes closed, then opened again to the shadows of an unfamiliar world. Before we went to the kitchen he gave me a tight fast hug.

Christina's short hair was mussed. She wore no make-up, but she looked beautiful with the sun shining softly on her pale face. She set down her fork as we came in.

"Who are you?"

"I'm Steve."

"You are? You're grown up! Yes, it is you! Still with Karen, always Karen. You never liked me."

"Christina..." he said. Either instinct or subconscious memory guided him to her side and he took her hand. "I'm not that little brat anymore."

She gazed at her small hand resting in his large one, until at last she looked up at him. "You were the biggest brat! But you could sure catch pollywogs down in the pond. Ones with legs, too. You gave Karen the good ones with legs."

"Didn't I give you any?"

"Mine aren't as good. Little front legs, that's all. No good ones with back legs. They're all in the bucket and some got out."

Steve leaned over, kissed Christina's forehead tenderly and repeated, "I'm not a brat now. We're friends now. You can trust me. We'll help each other. All right?"

She sighed shakily. "Can you stop them from coming after me?"

"Who?"

"Donald or Sonny. Or the old lady. They always come after me. They tell me not to come home anymore, but I had to come home and find Karen. I found her!"

"How did you get . . . home?"

"People give me a ride. I hitch."

"How far is it?"

"Oh, far! But I say I'm going to Tyrone and they know where it is."

Steve and I exchanged glances. I said softly, "The old lady—she means Daphne."

"What?"

I nodded. "Christina has a supply of keys to the house. Daphne doesn't know that, but there is some connection between the two of them. Steve, why would Daphne keep all this from me?"

"Or from me?" He straightened and slammed a fist into his palm. "Daphne thinks I'm guilty!"

"No—"

"I think she does!"

Christina was eating again. "Yes, you're guilty! I never got the good pollywogs. Why are you talking about Daphne? Do you know her?"

He winced. "Yeah. I know her."

"She gives me things. These jeans. She gave me these. If it wasn't for her I wouldn't have anything good to wear. I wouldn't have a TV or anything. Does she buy you things?''

Steve shook his head in confusion. I urged him away from Christina, to the other side of the kitchen. ''We've got to talk to Daphne, but we can't take Christina.''

''We can't both go and leave her here. Do you want me to stay? Will she stay with me?''

''I think so if I ask her to.''

''Daphne does think I'm guilty, dammit. Why else would she be taking care of one of the Saxons' daughters?''

''Maybe just to be kind.''

''Maybe. But the secrecy makes no sense.''

I turned to leave, anxious to confront Daphne about my sister. I had almost forgotten where Steve had been just now.

''Your meeting with Glen. What did he want?''

''To tell me I had no right and no cause to fire the sheriff. Dyer is planning to take it to court.''

''Can he?''

''Sure, but he can't win. Anyway, Glen is backing off because I decided to tell him what I know about the Saxon murder. He got a little upset. He said he remembers when I ran away. He was the one who gave our whereabouts away. We had a secret place at the river. Glen said we used to hide things there—I think he meant things he stole. Anyway, he was pressured into telling my mother where we were. He says he never knew my hiding had anything to do with the Saxons' deaths. The sheriff did a damn good job of sliding the whole thing under the rug.''

''I think Glen is dangerous,'' I said.

''Dangerous? How?''

"I don't trust him. He's betrayed you too many times."

"Daphne doesn't trust him, either—never has. But I could never see why. I guess we got into trouble together as kids, and because he was so much older he was probably my role model and led me into some rather heavy mischief."

"No doubt he did."

"No doubt. It was a long time ago, though. Karen, don't stay long at Daphne's, okay? Find out what you can and then get back, because somebody is bound to be looking for Christina. We need to talk about your options as soon as you can find out what the hell is going on. Take my car. It's parked behind yours."

On the short drive, I remembered Steve was an attorney and could advise us on Christina's rights. I also remembered what he seemed to have forgotten: Daphne had my mother's ring! Someone had stolen it and now she had it. Something else kept gnawing at me. By his own admission, and now by Steve's, Glen had been a thief as a child. Both he and Steve had hidden things somewhere on the river island—stolen things. And how had Daphne come by that ring? Could it ever have been stolen by her buddy Chuck Dyer, who was first on the scene?

Daphne had deliberately deceived me. So how to approach her now took some planning. I would have to trick her into believing I knew more than I actually did. That was what everyone feared, wasn't it? That I knew more than I actually did? Why else all the paranoia?

Daphne herself opened the door. To my relief the housekeeper was not in the house. Steve's grandmother seemed surprised, and not pleased to see me. My friendship with Steve was a threat to her, and now I had the gall to come alone.

"I must talk to you," I said.

Reluctantly she motioned me inside. "Where's Steve?"

"Not here. I have to talk to you alone."

We sat across from each other in the sitting room. My jeans were covered with dust from the floor of the Saxon house and my face was flushed, my eyes red rimmed. She couldn't help but notice the changes in me in the past two hours since I'd left here.

I began, "I've learned my identity, Mrs. Hayes. And I know I have a twin, Christina. I think it was rotten of you to deceive me."

She gazed at me. "I admit it was not good of me to deceive you. I hoped you'd leave never knowing. It's nothing personal, my dear. You just have no idea what Steve's mother and I went through in those months following the deaths of your parents. He doesn't remember, and I don't want him to."

"He's an adult now. He can handle it."

"Why should he have to? And he . . . doesn't know all the facts."

I stared at her. "You think he was guilty?"

"The sheriff still thinks so. In any case, I don't want any dust kicked up and you've been raising a storm of it ever since you got here. You must let it alone, Karen."

"You wanted me out of town so badly you resorted to voodoo, didn't you?"

She hesitated, then answered, "There is nothing I wouldn't do to protect Steve."

I felt like screaming. "Mrs. Hayes, I can't believe you think Steve was capable of murder!"

"Of course I don't think he was, and yet there is no doubt in my mind he saw Mrs. Saxon die at the hand of her husband. The poor child's mind could have snapped. This is what the police thought—he just went temporarily berserk. You didn't know him as a child. He was incorrigible, much of it thanks to his renegade cousin. There was bad blood in the Hadsell branch of the family—both Glen and Steve could be violent. They loved guns. And Steve's fingerprints..." She bit her lip. "I'm telling you, I do not want this matter dredged up. I simply won't stand for it."

"You've supported my sister all these years, haven't you?"

"How do you know that? Oh, my God! She's here again?"

"Why have you done it?"

"Because I could afford to and because I care."

"And because you think your grandson might be involved in her father's death?"

"The child was ill, horribly traumatized and an orphan. One does what one can to help."

I looked down at her hand.

"That diamond ring," I said. "Where did you get it?" Her expression changed abruptly. "What?"

"It was my mother's ring."

"It certainly was not! How dare you say such a thing!"

"I remember vividly when that same ring was on my mother's hand. How did you get it?"

"It's mine! It was a gift!"

"My father bought it for my mother. When I was in the house today, flashes of that day came back to me. It was her birthday and I was with him when he bought it for her." I only half remembered; I was filling in blank spaces with logic. Now intuition and my subconscious were taking over. Time was filling in, ever so slowly. Thanks to Chrissy.

Her eyes grew suddenly wild. "He didn't buy it for her! He bought it for me!"

A hideous silence came down over us. Too stunned to react, I sat there as frozen as a chunk of ice. We stared at each other. I began to tremble violently. Swallowing, I prayed for strength.

"What did you say?"

She was shaken. "A friend bought it for me."

"Was that friend my father?"

"No!"

"You just said it was! Who *did* Wayne buy the ring for?"

Her eyes closed slowly. "For me."

"And then he gave it to her?"

"No!"

"I remember when he gave it to her. I remember him placing it on her finger." Actually I remembered no such thing, but I was moving on pure instinct now. Any woman could have recognized what I saw in Daphne's eyes. Her eyes gave everything away. And my goading was pushing her to the brink.

Daphne and Wayne Saxon—lovers? Had *he* taken the ring from my mother's hand? This thought was more than I could bear. Desperately fighting back tears, I knew if I could push Daphne over that precarious edge of control she was balancing on, I'd find out the truth.

I persisted, "Mary was wearing the ring when she died."

She glared at me as if she wanted to kill me. "It was me he loved, not her! Me!"

I took control of my reeling mind and braced myself. Gasping, I said, "Did you take the ring from Mary's hand?"

Daphne's eyes glazed over. "I had a right to! It was mine! He meant it for me!"

"Dear God," I breathed. "It was you. You were so jealous of my mother, you killed her?"

Daphne jumped to her feet. Before I realized what she was doing, she had dived for a drawer in the tall Oriental chest and pulled out a handgun. She aimed it straight at my head.

"I can use this!" she threatened. "As you know I can use this! You'll never be able to tell anyone. I'll make sure of it."

I tried to swallow, but my mouth had gone dry. I had recognized Daphne's vulnerability and goaded her on purpose. But I had been too dense to realize this was an unstoppable woman, who took whatever she wanted, at any cost.

Once she had wanted my father! He had chosen his wife over her instead—and they both had died.

"It was his kids..." She was muttering, the gun trembling in her hand. "You and your sister. If it hadn't been for you two little darlings, he'd have left her. You ruined my life then and you're trying to do it again!"

I heard my flat lifeless voice say, "You killed them." As I stared at the gun, I could barely comprehend the danger I was in. A gun was just a small cold metal thing.

I continued, "And the house was full of children at the time...."

"How was I supposed to know the girls were home? They should have been in preschool like on other days. And Steve was supposed to be in school, too, the little renegade. He came in through the upstairs window when he heard you screaming—and after being told a thousand times not to climb on the high branches of that tree!

I left the house barely in time, just before he might have seen me."

"You shot them, Daphne?"

"I had to. Wayne was going to stay with her. Betray me, when I loved him. No one betrays me." Her voice had become so calm I knew she planned to kill me.

I said, "They'll figure everything out if you kill me. Steve knows about the ring."

"The ring?" She reached down and wrenched it from her finger with a violent jerk. "Without this, it's your word against mine. No one will find it—ever!" With a quick flick of her wrist, she tossed the ring through the open window. I saw only a brilliant flash as the sun caught the sparkle of diamonds.

My stomach dropped. It was a soggy marsh out there. The ring would sink into the soft black mud and be gone forever. And for the loss of it, she would hate me even more.

"Now," she said. "Move over by the window away from the rug. I will say you threatened me. They will believe me. They always do. My word is gold here."

She could actually think of the damn carpet! The woman was insane. I was not, and I had no intention of cooperating.

A movement in the door caught my eye. Instinct prevented me from turning, for the slightest movement on my part might cause her to squeeze the trigger. I stood stone still.

"Move!" she demanded.

With her back to him, she didn't see Steve enter. My knees were threatening to buckle. I held my breath. If she heard anything—the least noise from him—she would surely fire! Steve knew it, too.

He was directly behind her now. His voice boomed, "Hit the floor, Karen!" as he swooped in and pushed Daphne's arm hard from underneath, causing the shot to fire toward the ceiling. Before I realized what was happening he had the weapon in his own hand and was tossing it behind him, far down the hallway.

His grandmother swooned and fell into his arms. She looked up at him. "Oh, Steve! Karen threatened to kill me... I was terrified..."

"I heard everything," he said. And to me, "I got worried when you didn't come right back, but I sure as hell didn't expect..." His voice broke with emotion.

Picking myself up from the floor, I wobbled to a chair on rubber knees. "Christina?"

"She's with Kimberly—I called her. I don't know how I knew you'd be in trouble, but I did." He was staring at his grandmother as he lowered her limp body onto the couch. "I think subconsciously I remembered more than I knew," he said to her. "I've always known you were dangerous, Daphne."

She seemed barely to hear him and was looking glassily past him. "Mud! Mud on my Persian rug!"

Skipper Flash was bouncing into the room through the open doors, leaving a trail of muddy black footprints. I thought, It was true. She was insane. Or at the least she was incapable of comprehending what had just happened.

"Steve," she scolded, "you must control that animal!"

He looked at me incredulously, then knelt beside her. "Daphne, I can't believe it. You got away with a double murder by letting the sheriff put the blame on me."

"You weren't supposed to be there! I didn't plan that."

"But you planned to kill them and make it look like a murder/suicide, and you succeeded."

"I had no choice! We belonged together. I loved him. No man leaves me, especially for a young twit like her."

"She was his wife."

"She was twenty-six years old! And he was over forty! He was my age—he'd be old now, wouldn't he? And she would be only fifty."

It was hard for Steve to look at me; he didn't know how much of this I'd be able to take. My brain was so numb by now, I felt very little. I only wanted the truth. Finally the truth.

"Tell me exactly what happened," I said, moving next to Steve.

"What is there to say?" She scowled.

"Tell us!" Steve demanded.

She simply glared. Something had snapped, though; the second I had mentioned the ring, she'd gone limp. There was no fight in her now, as though Daphne had always known it would come to this someday.

"You might as well tell us," Steve insisted, "because the police will easily be able to put it together with what Karen remembers."

"You're threatening me."

"That's right."

"You can't. The statute of limitations will protect me. Everyone will. Anyway, you already know what happened. I went in the front door. She was wearing the ring. I took it after I fired the gun because it was mine. Wayne was back in his office. One of the twins was screaming by the time I got back there. He started coming for me, so I fired. Then I heard you yelling, Steve, screaming at the girls not to come down the stairs. Karen stayed on the stairs like you told her, but Christina followed you down.

When you heard the second and third shots, you ran toward the back. I barely got out in time. Why you picked up the gun, I don't know, but you evidently did pick it up. I could hear the girls screaming, and you screaming back. When the police arrived, no one was in the house but Christina.''

"She wouldn't come with us!" I cried, as the scene opened up inside my mind. "We begged her and she got as far as the back porch, and then she turned around and ran back in. It was Christina who set the fire!"

Daphne's voice steadied. She looked up at her grandson. "There is nothing you can do about this now," she said. "Karen always did everything you wanted her to, always. She still will. You can't turn me in to the police. I'm seventy years old. You wouldn't dare do anything about this. Karen will have to get out of town. I'll deny everything. No one would ever believe this story, and you know it."

Skipper, failing to get any attention from Steve, kept rubbing against me. I tried to push him away, until I realized he was trying to put something in my hand.

"The ring!" I said. "Skipper has the diamond ring!"

Steve turned. "I'll be damned! Skip, you pirate! He must have been nosing around under the window when the thing went flying out." Steve looked at his grandmother. "Everybody in town has seen you wear this ring. What did you do? Claim you bought it in the estate sale?"

"No one ever asked. They didn't know it came from him. He had just given it to her. No one knew then, and no one would believe Karen now."

"I'm going to call the sheriff," he said.

"You can't! I'm an old lady! I've protected you all these years—"

"You've protected yourself, dammit! You're...I can't believe it! You're a murderer, for God's sake! You'd have killed Karen if I hadn't been here."

"No, I wouldn't have!"

"I think you would have."

Tears formed in her pale blue eyes. "If you turn me in it's the same as killing me. And killing yourself, in a different way. The scandal will never die down. Never!"

He brushed his hair nervously from his forehead. "You might as well have killed Christina, too, that day, for what that horror has done to her."

"I've supported her ever since. I've arranged for the best care she could get. All these years."

"That hardly makes up for it!"

Daphne began to cry. She leaned into her hands and sobbed the loss of her grandson—the only thing on earth that really mattered to her. Steve's respect, probably his love, were gone. I sat too numb to feel anything. Steve's face was a mask of agony. I just wanted out of there. I wanted to go to Christina.

Skipper and I left the two of them there. Steve was still kneeling beside her. My mother's ring was in Steve's hand, fury was in his eyes, and I could almost feel the pain that was in his heart.

KIMBERLY ROSE when Skip and I walked into Steve's kitchen. She looked at me with concern and curiosity; I must have looked awful. But for Christina's sake, she only smiled.

"Christina has been telling me about the old days. About the ballerina paper dolls and the toy piano. Is everything all right, Karen?"

"Yes, fine." I was afraid to look at Kim.

"Good. I'll go then. I'm sure you want to talk. You can count on me, Karen. I won't tell anybody you two are here."

"Thanks. We appreciate that."

I sat down next to my sister and took her hand. "What an incredible day this is, Chrissy! Finding you is like a miracle! It's finding myself."

"Yes." She smiled. "I knew your memory was gone, Karen. Otherwise you'd have found me sooner. I knew that."

"Twins know things about each other, don't they?"

"We used to have a lot of secrets."

"I want to know everything we used to do. We'll sit and talk for hours—for years—Chrissy. No one will ever separate us again."

Tears spilled from her eyes and she grasped my hands as if she would never let go.

Thirty minutes later Steve came in looking as though he'd been through a war. He was holding a sheet of paper, which he handed to me along with the diamond ring.

"The Saxon house is yours," he said stiffly. "I don't know what good it is to you, but it's yours. The Hayes building downtown, where the department store and the drugstore are located, and the offices above—that building belongs to Christina. It's worth more than any other building in town and it brings in a good steady income. I'll manage it for her until you find somebody else to do it."

"I don't understand," Christina said.

My eyes were brimming. I had thought there were no tears left in me, but maybe there would never be an end to them. "It's a gift from Mrs. Hayes," I said.

"A whole building? Why?"

"She's old and doesn't need it anymore," Steve explained. "And she wants you to have it."

"How nice! I want to thank her!"

"It isn't necessary," he said.

He looked at me. "I suppose you both want to just get out of this nightmare of a town as soon as possible."

"This is our home!" Christina protested.

"It isn't our home anymore," I said. "Chrissy, it doesn't matter where we live as long as we have each other."

"I envy you getting out of here," Steve said in a weak voice, feeling the burden of responsibility for the agony his grandmother had caused. "I'll help any way I can."

"And who is going to help you?" I asked him.

"Help me? I don't need any help."

"Really? Your life has turned completely upside down and you can handle that okay, can you?"

"I'll be fine," he said.

"Oh, yes. You're great at coping. Add on another layer of bitterness, Steve. The layers have formed a nice thick crust. Crust rusted and turned to armor."

He looked at me strangely. "It's you and Christina I'm worried about."

Christina tugged at my arm. "Kimberly made lemonade. Do you want some?"

"Sure." I smiled. "We both do."

She went across to the refrigerator. Steve and I stepped out of the room, out of her hearing. I whispered, "I've loved you all my life, haven't I?"

"It would seem so," he answered.

"I came back to you."

This brought a sad crooked smile. "I was still here. The minute I saw you something in me remembered."

"I never really left you."

"I know."

"Steve . . . I don't want to leave you now."

This shocked him. "How could you stay in Tyrone? How could you ever stay here, Karen?"

"Why not? The few who know who I am will never talk about it."

"You're a dreamer."

"Of course I am—we've established that. But I'm not fragile. I can deal with events of so long ago. I have Christina. I'm a thousand times richer than when I came and found the two of you again. Don't you want me to stay?"

"I don't know . . . what I want."

"Oh, Steve! Do I need an ice pick to chip off the layers of armor to find that boy who loved me?"

His head jerked up. I had never seen the expression in his eyes that I saw there now—except maybe once at the river.

"The boy who loved me," I whispered. "The boy who knows me. The boy who always protected me, trusted me."

"I think that boy...is still here," he said haltingly. "He loved you when he was eight years old . . ."

"And I was five."

His shoulders relaxed. His eyes changed colors as the shadows left them, as he allowed himself to admit that our love was real. "It's a long time loving each other," he admitted. "Too long to let it go." He took my hand. "Maybe we'd better not let it go. . . ."

"There'll be time for mending," I said.

"And time for building."

Steve drew me close and I felt his strength become my strength and his needs become mine. I felt his heart become willing at last to let my love in—not for the first time in our lives but for the second time. And the love was still as pure as it had been those many, many years ago, when once a little boy had loved me.

Epilogue

One Year Later

My new design was inspired from the open wings of a hawk in flight. I was leaning over the drawing table in my studio when Steve came in hot and sweating and peered over my shoulder at the sketches.

"Will it be in gold or silver?"

"Silver. Do you like it?"

He nodded. "I'm proud as hell of you. Want to hear Glen's comment when I told him you were opening a shop in New York? He asked how an artist of your caliber could end up with a small-town klutz like me."

I added a bit of shading to one of the drawings. "When are you and Cuz Glen going to break down and express your appreciation for each other?"

"What fun would we have in that?"

"None," I conceded. "We wouldn't want to break the bickering tradition. You're dripping with perspiration. Did you finish the roof?"

"No. Only two idiots of our league would attempt to repair a roof on a day as hot as this. We've been baked alive."

"Where's Glen now? Did he leave?"

"He grabbed a shower and my clothes and took off for the Pawnee Saloon to talk about his recent divorce and his RV-park project."

I laughed. "Your jeans don't fit him. He won't be able to breathe."

"That's what cuz said—he could only hold half a beer in my jeans."

"That's encouraging. Everything is, Steve. I can't believe you guys finally reached a compromise. Are you happy with it?"

"It was really no compromise. I got what I wanted. By turning twenty miles of river into a wildlife sanctuary we control the camping. The river is safe, the geese are happy, and Glen is finally convinced we're too isolated for attracting more tourists than an RV park will accommodate. There'll be a lot of summer visitors, though, if we do this right. Plenty of revenue, and Glen will finally make some real money from his land." Steve smeared dirt on his face when he wiped his brow. "I need a beer and a shower, in that order."

"Speaking of showers, Kimberly's baby shower is tonight. The house will be filled with women."

"Sounds like a good night for me to call a town-council meeting to go over plans for the retirement home." He leaned over and nuzzled my cheek. "It'll be your turn for the baby shower next. Have you announced it yet?"

"No. Shall I announce it tonight?"

"Sure! Let's announce it to the world. I'll go ring the church bell."

"Of course you will."

"I will! That's what my father did. It's a family tradition. Where's Chrissy?"

"Fussing with the table setting in the dining room. I knew it was a great idea to have this shower while she's visiting. She loves parties."

"Then we'll plan a smash of a bash next month. You two are long overdue for a shared birthday party." He kissed my temple and left the room unbuttoning his shirt and cursing the heat.

Steve had been wonderful with Christina. She visited us one weekend every month, and next week she would leave the hospital and move into the lovely apartment we had made for her in the upper northeast wing of the house.

At first Steve had balked over living in what used to be the Saxon house. But he was intrigued when the ghost sightings persisted. And when Chrissy and I were deep into our redecorating plans, he got caught up in the challenges and agreed that the place could be restored to the most beautiful Victorian mansion in this half of the state. It was well on its way to being that. And all of Tyrone believed it was still haunted.

To this day we hadn't found any explanation for the strange glow that appeared in the upper hallways on certain nights. We didn't know what caused the whispering sounds in two of the rooms. Chrissy had no fear of the ghosts; she seemed to welcome them, so in this we trusted her. Whatever the presence, it was friendly. Some day perhaps we would be able to talk more about it, but it was still too soon....

This late-summer afternoon was too soon. In my study I had lost track of the time. Now, glancing at the clock on the wall, I put aside my work.

From the hall I could hear Chrissy and the maid discussing china and silver. I hurried upstairs, peeled off my shorts and shirt and was standing in my underwear by the bed when Steve emerged from the bathroom, naked and dripping. He pulled me playfully into his arms.

He said, "There's time..."

"The guests will be arriving in less than two hours."

"Who cares?"

His body next to mine, soapy clean and hard, was too persuasive for me to resist and he knew it. "Right," I agreed. "Who cares?"

IN THE AFTERGLOW of our lovemaking, I propped myself on my elbow and brushed Steve's still-damp hair from his eyes. "Will you tell Daphne about the baby?"

"No."

"It will be her only grandchild."

"She won't be a part of your life, nor mine. We went far beyond our obligations to her just to keep her bloody damn secret."

"We kept her secret for our sake, too."

"Yeah, I know. But still, it haunts me to the point I have to force it out of my mind. Daphne's health has been failing since last summer. She plans to go to a nursing home. She's alone, but that was the choice she made when she took it upon herself to destroy your family. She got off better than she deserves."

The subject of Daphne was never really resolved. For weeks before our wedding Steve hadn't been able to let go of the fact that she might have murdered me. The people of Tyrone buzzed about why Daphne wasn't at our wedding, even though she feigned illness. We rarely talked about her now. There wasn't much left to say. She lived in a self-induced hell caused by losing Steve; we couldn't have changed that even if we'd tried. We didn't try.

Sheriff Dyer called on her from time to time. We think they were lovers once. The few others, like Henry

Paulson, who were involved in the cover-up, sensed something horribly wrong in the rift between Steve and his grandmother. In the end their loyalties were to him.

Ervin Eckles was an effective sheriff. He and Kim had married last August, a month before Steve and I. Glen and Steve got smashed beyond reason the night before our wedding, and in a haze of sentimentality decided blood was thicker than either water or whiskey and buried their differences with toasts to future ventures together. Glen, too, sensed something had changed. I think he suspected the truth, because it wasn't like him never to ask.

So Cuz Glen stood beside Steve at our wedding. Chrissy stood by me, radiant in a gown of pink satin. She kept the satin dress in my closet and wore it often because she loved it so.

As Steve and I lay on our bed under a ceiling fan, hating to get up, tree branches brushed our bedroom window. "Wind is coming up," he said.

"For a minute I thought it was the ghost."

He smiled. "You were right about the house. I'm glad we decided to live here—even with the ghost."

"We have Chrissy to thank for that. She has more courage than the two of us combined. We wanted to run from the past. She convinced us it was better to accept it."

"Honey," he said gently, "she's still stuck in it."

"I know. But she's so much better."

"Thanks to you."

"And to you."

I forced myself to get up. By the time I finished my shower Steve had dozed off. He'd been on the roof since morning, baking, as he said, and he was exhausted. I watched him sleep, filled to bursting with my love for him.

The fragrance of magnolia blossoms floated through the open windows this summer evening. Crickets chirped and the night birds warbled sweetly.

I descended the stairway under the light of a crystal chandelier. The house spoke to me as it had done so often since I had come home to live. This poor house so long abandoned...so lonely...like us. It had deserved another chance. With Chrissy guiding us, we took back only the good from the past and built on that.

Hardly anyone in Tyrone remembers the Saxons. This is the Hayes house now. The town our children grow up in won't remember the Saxons at all, but there will always be whisperings about the ghost.

Steve and I will tell our children a strange true story when they are old enough to hear it. The secrets of Tyrone will live on with them and their children after them.

Why not let the secrets die? Because we are witnesses to the fact that children deserve to know the truth. The secrets hidden in this house are our children's legacy. And the house they will grow up in is already so refurbished with love that even its ghosts are gentle.

throughout, adding words to the sentence.